DOCTOR IN THE SWIM

Richard Gordon

DOCTOR IN THE SWIM

DOUBLEDAY & COMPANY, INC.
Garden City, New York

DOCTOR IN THE SWIM

Chapter One

"To my mind, flying in an airplane is just like being ill in a hospital," I expanded toward the beautiful girl in the next seat.

"In hospital! Rather a gruesome comparison, isn't it?"

"Not a bit." I was becoming rather witty after the third free martini. "In both you're firmly immobilized by the authorities, you have to balance your dinner on your knees, there's nothing whatever to do except read magazines and snooze, and you're attended by a bunch of highly trained young females who always turn out about half as pretty as you hoped."

The girl laughed.

"Furthermore," I ended, "I bet everyone goes into an airplane or a hospital half-wondering if they'll ever get out of either again alive. Another martini?"

"What, another? Oh, dear me, no. I never have more than one before dinner."

"But our dinner's a good five hundred miles ahead," I pointed out.

"Well . . ." The girl hesitated. "Perhaps if I pretended it was only my first . . ."

"Pretend it's your birthday instead."

I pressed the little plastic knob over my head. We were forty thousand feet above the Atlantic, and it was becoming very cozy.

I hadn't noticed the girl while I was scrambling aboard the plane in New York. It's impossible to notice anything at all while you're scrambling aboard a plane, what with the people gargling at you through the loudspeakers, the bossy girls in uniform who seem to imagine you're lost from an outing for handicapped children, and trying to remember where you've stuffed all those vital little bits of paper you collect at airports like bookies' tickets on Derby Day. I'd simply jostled up the gangway steps thinking only how I'd like a word with the cunning fellows who draw the airline advertisements—you know the ones, depicting the customers lolling about inside, all handsome chaps making light conversation to pretty girls, with a dear old couple beaming in the background to show the whole business is no more unnerving than a trip on the subway.

Personally, I find with modern high-speed flying you first spend half a day sitting on a little plastic airport chair wondering if that was really your suitcase you saw disappearing toward Bangkok. Then when they finally manage to get all the engines working at once, you discover yourself rubbing elbows aboard with some fat chap who speaks no known language and insists on lighting shocking cigars, or in the middle of a bunch of kids being sick all over you, like the day excursion to Margate. So you can understand how I blessed my luck when the prettiest girl I had seen in my life simply murmured, "Is this seat occupied?" and moved in beside me for the next eight hours.

Being an Englishman, one would naturally not immediately strike up a conversation, even if one found oneself sitting next to Cleopatra all togged up for the Nile. But I'll say this for airplanes—next to a ship's lifeboat there's nothing like them for getting to know your next-door passenger. All that tangling up of the safety belts, and pressing the seat knob that throws you flat on your back, and adjusting the nozzle that shoots the jet of ice-cold air down your neck, makes powerfully for what the Americans call "Togetherness." And that isn't to mention the free martinis.

"What do you think of New York?" I asked, before the girl had time to read through the gay little pamphlet they issue telling you what to do when the plane crashes. "The magnificent skyline, and all that?"

She glanced through the window, where Manhattan was poking its fingers at us through the clouds.

"A freak," she said.

"But a magnificent freak."

The girl nodded. "I suppose you could call it the Venice of the twentieth century."

We ran into one of the clouds, and nothing being so un-interesting to look at as clouds from the inside, she turned and remarked New York was all very well but it was nice to be going home to London, and I agreed it was nice to be going home to London, too. Then she said she'd been staying with relatives in Poughkeepsie, and I gave a little laugh and said I always thought that was a preposterous name, and she gave a little laugh, too, and said well they were preposterous rel-atives. We were soon enjoying a jet-propelled chumminess, particularly when the hostess responded to the little plastic knob to bring my fourth martini, with that air of the vicar's daughter handing round the tea, which somehow never escapes the girls on British airlines.

It was then I suddenly had a rummy feeling. I'd met my beautiful traveling companion somewhere before.

I edged a better look while the aircraft's captain, who seemed to be enjoying a mouthful of humbugs, came on the intercom to wish us good evening, reassure us he knew where he was going, and mention it was pouring with rain in London. She was a little dark girl in a little dark dress with a diamond spar-kling here and there, and the way she smelt alone must have cost a packet. I was about to oil the hinges of my memory by remarking surely we'd met somewhere before, but quickly decided against it. The girl might have been some famous film star traveling on the quiet. She might have been one of those models you get to know pretty well going up and down the escalators on the Underground. And, I reflected with a cautious sigh, this imperfect world is alive with girls, bookies, beaks, and bank managers one never wants to meet again.

"Have you been over to the States on pleasure or business?" asked the girl, as the captain clicked off.

I twiddled the stem of my martini glass.

"Actually, I've been attending a rather important medical congress in New York."

"Really?" She switched on her lovely eyes. "Then you're a doctor?"

I gave a professional little nod.

She sighed. "Yours must be an absolutely fascinating life."

"Well, it has its moments."

"What is it you specialize in?"

"Specialize?"

"I mean, you must really be a terribly important specialist, going for conferences all the way to New York."

"I'm afraid I'm a nonstarter in the specialist stakes myself," I admitted. "But I was accompanying a rather important professional pundit. A London surgeon, name of Sir Lancelot Spratt."

"Oh, I've heard of him," said the girl at once. "Isn't he always in the papers, treating dukes and cabinet ministers and film stars?"

I nodded. "That's the one."

I'd often suspected that after attending particularly distinguished households Sir Lancelot pretended his car wouldn't start until someone had taken his photograph.

"Yes, he wanted to operate on my father once. He was terribly persuasive about it."

I'd often suspected Sir Lancelot believed nothing did anyone quite so much good as a really decent operation.

"But Daddy wouldn't let him. I remember there was quite a scene."

We sat for a moment listening to the woosh of the jets, my memory being violently elbowed by my subconscious. I supposed the girl might have been one of my patients. But she didn't seem one I was likely to forget, particularly if she'd had anything wrong below the clavicles. Perhaps I'd once passed her the canapés at some party. Perhaps I'd once told her the way to Marble Arch. Or perhaps, I reflected, noticing my martini eyeing me severely with its olive, I'd simply got to the stage when all girls were starting to look the same.

At that moment the vicar's daughter reappeared with the dinner. Conversation is, of course, impossible while you're trying to sort out all that caviar, fruit tart, roast duck, peppermint fudge, Stilton cheese, and orchids mixed up on the same little plastic tray. I was still busy prizing open the packets of salt and pepper and getting at my knife and fork wrapped in sterilized cellophane like a pair of surgical instruments, when the girl remarked:

"I think Daddy was feeling rather peeved with doctors at the time. You see, my brother wanted to be a doctor, but somehow he never managed to get into one of the medical schools. The poor lamb's so terribly shy at interviews, he always gets torpedoed by the first question with a psychological warhead."

"Your brother—!" I exclaimed.

I stared at her. The penny dropped, with the noise of the tinkling of little silver bells.

"Good lord." I smiled. "Where are the pigtails?"

The girl looked startled. "I beg your pardon?"

"The pigtails. The ones I used to pull." I decided it best not to mention her spots. "That summer at Whortleton-on-Sea."

She turned up the eyes to full candle power.

"You couldn't possibly be Gaston Grimsdyke—?"

"I could."

"And you became a doctor—?"

"In the fullness of time, yes."

She gave a little gasp. "Well, fancy that!"

"And you couldn't be Lucy Squiffington?"

"But of course I am."

"Well, fancy *that!*"

We both burst out laughing. I pressed the little plastic knob again.

My affair with Lucy, like some of the world's great passions, had blossomed delicately on a patch of prickly dislike. I happened to pinch her bucket, so she hit me over the ear with her spade. Then she kidnapped the special crab I was keeping to put in her brother's bed, so I slid an ice cream down her neck. The tiff went on for ages—quite three whole sunlit days—until the afternoon I first discovered that a chap can go too far, when I jumped on her sand castle with the real battlements and launched poor Lucy into a sea of tears. Luckily, I shortly afterwards had a chance to display my finer qualities by removing a bee from her neck, even though I did happen to know myself it was one of the sort that didn't sting. After that, I showed her my collection of dead men's fingers and she gave me a jellyfish, and there was no holding us.

"What on earth is brother George up to now?" I asked, after we'd had a bit of a giggle while the vicar's daughter hustled up with the buckshee champagne.

"George? Oh, he's doing terribly well. He's one of those atomic scientists you keep reading about in the papers. He's engaged in frightfully secret research for the government somewhere in the middle of the country."

"What, old George?" I exclaimed.

I was surprised. These atomic chaps have to pack heavyweight brains, and when we were at school together young Squiffy was what they called a late starter, though I myself fancied he was an early finisher as well. We were on marble-sharing terms, which accounted for his invitation to Whortleton, and in fact we sailed up the academic stream together until he became shipwrecked on Boyle's Law and was told by the beaks that his only chance of getting into a hospital was being run over by a bus.

"I think you'd find George a changed person now," observed Lucy, a little sternly.

"I'm sure he's got just the touch for the government's atoms," I added quickly. I supposed that Boyle's Law was now as outdated as a forge and bellows, anyway. "I only meant that I hope he keeps the secrets well locked up."

I remembered I'd once confided in the chap that I slept in my socks, and it was all round the school before mid-morning break.

"George never says a single word about his work to anyone. Not even to me, and we've shared secrets all our lives. But it must be frightfully important, because the poor lamb's becoming quite nervy and edgy under the strain. I worry over him awfully, sometimes. But what about you, Gaston?" She laid a little hand on my arm. "All sorts of exciting things must have happened since you bought me that stick of rock on the departure platform at Whortleton. That was terribly nice of you, by the way."

"Not a bit. Hope you enjoyed it."

"I suppose you've got some tremendously important practice in London?"

"My practice, I'm afraid, is even more unexacting than Dr. Watson's," I told her, not wishing to go into it too deeply at the time.

Lucy looked puzzled. "But if you attended this important meeting in New York as a doctor—"

"In New York I wasn't a doctor. I was a ruddy nursemaid." I sighed. "And what I attended was less a medical meeting than the breeziest Anglo-American rumpus since the Boston Tea Party."

"But Gaston, this all sounds terribly intriguing."

"I'll tell you about it," I declared. "Once I feel strong enough." I reached for the little plastic knob again.

Chapter Two

My trip to New York was a fringe benefit from ghost-writing Sir Lancelot Spratt's autobiography, which, under the title of *Fifty Years of Sport and Surgery* (he'd turned down my suggestion of *With Rod and Gun Down the Alimentary Canal*), had recently been published in London at fifty bob and sold briskly among his relatives. But the old boy was tickled enough seeing his name in print, and sent me a very civil invitation to celebrate the literary event with a weekend at his country house in Wales.

I was surprised at the summons to Wales, because all the time I was writing the book Sir Lancelot was grumbling he couldn't afford to keep up a country place now he'd retired from the surgical staff of St. Swithin's, still with a wife and government to support. And though Sir Lancelot himself was eager to spend the rest of his days up to the waist in freezing water outwitting fish, or causing nasty accidents to the local birds, Lady Spratt much preferred to get the provisions more conventionally by telephoning Harrods.

I was in for an even bigger surprise on the bright May afternoon I drove my 1930 Bentley along the banks of the River Usk, where it chortles and jostles among the Black Mountains as gaily as a bunch of kids getting out of school. I turned through Sir Lancelot's front gates to see a middle-aged chap in shorts dashing down the long drive, with the surgeon himself in tweed knickerbockers and deer-stalker hat in close pursuit.

"Stop that man!" shouted Sir Lancelot. "Stop him, I say."

Quickly deciding the chap in shorts had been interrupted rifling the cutlery, I jammed on the brakes, leapt from the car, and grabbed him as he was ducking into the shrubbery.

"And so, Horsham," demanded Sir Lancelot, thundering up, "you have decided to discharge yourself, have you?"

The culprit, a weedy little fellow, all ears and kneecaps, could only stand and gasp.

"You might have paid me the courtesy of mentioning the matter. I could have made the necessary arrangements and saved you the embarrassment of attempting to hitchhike your way back to London in the garb of an underdressed Boy Scout."

"I—I'm sorry, Sir Lancelot," the fugitive managed to wheeze. "I don't know what came over me. Really, I don't. I just cut and ran, that's all."

Sir Lancelot stood stroking his beard. "I am inclined to suspect that you merely wished to avoid your afternoon's treatment."

"I would like to remind you who you are addressing," said the weedy chap, trying to draw himself up.

"As far as I am concerned I am addressing a blood pressure several points above normal and a physique several points below it, a muscular system exercised far too little and an alimentary system exercised far too much. Though if you would care for me to telephone," he added generously, "I can have your Rolls and chauffeur dispatched at once and you will still be in time for a late supper at the Caprice. It is a matter of supreme indifference to myself whether you remain here or not. Particularly as fees paid in advance are not returnable."

"I shall not dine at the Caprice tonight," said the weedy chap, with dignity, though salivating a good deal. "I shall stick it out, Sir Lancelot. I realize it is all for my own good."

"Excellent. Though if you break any more of the rules, Horsham, I fear I shall be obliged to invite you for a chat in my study after supper. Now kindly report to the sergeant major for your treatment at once."

"Who on earth was that, sir?" I asked, feeling mystified, as the defaulter padded off.

"Good afternoon, Grimsdyke," Sir Lancelot greeted me affably. "Pleasant to see you again. That? Oh, that was Lord Horsham."

"Lord Horsham?"

"Yes, Chairman of the City and Suburban Bank. Got nasty breath and fallen arches."

This seemed even more mysterious. Though I couldn't feel sorry for the chap any longer, his underlings on several occasions having totally failed to see the joke about my overdraft.

"Perhaps you will give me a lift to my own front door?" asked Sir Lancelot. "As you know," he explained, climbing into the car, "like most of the luckless possessors of the only houses in the country worth owning, I was recently faced with the prospect of an estate agent's board decorating the front gate."

I nodded. "I was going to suggest, sir, you get rather aristocratic and throw the place open at half-a-crown a go."

"I thought of that, but I didn't much like the prospect of spotty children sucking lollipops all over my flower beds."

"Or wiping their fingers on the priceless heirlooms."

"Being a self-made man, I unfortunately possess no heirlooms except my father's operating instruments. Though I have, over the years, collected in preservative spirit abdominal organs removed from many interesting and prominent people. I felt these would make an interesting exhibit, at a small extra charge. Not many people have the opportunity of inspecting a former prime minister's kidney," he mused as we reached the porch. "But my wife was for some reason much against the idea. She had become very conservative in her ways lately."

I felt this would have given the customers a change from all those portraits of the ancestors, but I didn't see where it led to the weedy chap in the shrubbery.

"Then I hit on the brilliant notion of turning my home into a rest clinic," Sir Lancelot added.

"A rest clinic, sir?"

So far the place struck me about as restful as jail.

"Yes, a clinic for overworked business executives. You read your papers, Grimsdyke? You must be aware that our modern businessman is as grossly overtaxed physically as fiscally. They keep gathering for deeply depressing lectures by eminent cardiologists, telling them how soon they'll drop dead and to live on a diet of sunflower seeds and yoghurt. Perfectly disgusting."

"But surely it's the great health problem of the age, sir?" I swung my bag from the back seat.

"It's no problem at all," answered Sir Lancelot briefly. "They simply eat and drink too much, smoke like the borough incinerator, and get no exercise beyond winding up their alarm clocks before dropping into bed stuffed to the eyeballs with barbiturates. Here we try to restore the natural environment of the human animal. Come and inspect the afternoon treatment."

Sir Lancelot led me through a gap in the shrubbery toward the lawn. A dozen more middle-aged chaps in running shorts were trotting briskly up and down, while a red-faced man in a track suit, resembling an international front-row forward who'd just been fouled in the scrimmage, stood and roared directions at them.

"My patients," explained Sir Lancelot proudly, "include three stockbrokers, two ennobled brewers, and a couple of take-over bidders who developed a neurosis when they attempted to take over each other. See the little chap struggling to keep up? He's one of the Income Tax Commissioners. I believe he gets bullied shockingly."

The surgeon paused, while the patients started knee-bends at the double.

"Observe the bald patient, whose shoulders would disgrace a bag of jelly-babies. That's Arnold Quellsby, the dramatic critic on the Sunday papers. Chronic dyspepsia and melancholia. I was nearly obliged to expell him from the clinic when I discovered him guzzling fruitcake in his bedroom. Smuggled in a parcel of socks, by some famous actress who no doubt wishes to curry favor with him. However, I relented. The poor fellow is not yet nearly strong enough to face our contemporary drama. He has terrible rows with that television impressario next to him."

I noticed a little fat fellow resembling a freshly poached red mullet.

"I advised them to ask the sergeant major for the gloves and have it out in the gym after tea. Do them both a power of good. The moral treatment here is quite as important as the physical, I believe."

A point was worrying me.

"How on earth do you manage to make the patients stay?" I asked.

Sir Lancelot laughed. "My dear feller, I simply charge them a hundred guineas a week. You'd be surprised what people will put up with, if only they have to pay enough for it. Though I do, of course," he added, "take the precaution of confiscating all their clothes and hiding them. We follow a perfectly simple regimen here," the surgeon continued as we stepped toward the house. "Up at six, bed at nine, starvation diet, cold baths, and readings from the classics in the evenings. It's remarkable the change you can see in a managing director in a fortnight."

I suppose I showed a sudden chilly feeling that the local rules might apply to visitors as well.

"My guests naturally enjoy their roast duck and claret,"

the surgeon reassured me, "while my patients have *Bleak House* and cocoa next door. I fancy even your cousin Miles was impressed by my efforts here when he escaped from his surgical treadmill for some fishing last weekend. Do you see much of him in town these days?"

"Our treadmills are rather separated, sir."

"H'm. I fancy it was Miles who brought my work to the notice of Dr. Lee Archbold during his recent visit to St. Swithin's. You know Archbold, of course?"

"You mean the American cardiologist you keep seeing getting in and out of airplanes in *Life?*"

Sir Lancelot nodded. "In the United States they make an even bigger fuss about executives' health, American businessmen enjoying the widespread admiration and affection reserved in this country only for dogs. Archbold has courteously asked me to New York as British delegate to the coming conference of the Wall Street Health Movement. The invitation is timely, as I feel inclined to close the clinic for a short holiday. Besides, my wife," Sir Lancelot explained after a pause, "is returning from a stay in Majorca, and I feel it would be best if she did not find it in full swing. I have a feeling that I overlooked mentioning its existence to her."

He paused as the inmates trotted past us on the heels of the sergeant major, off for a healthy two-mile run.

"I should be greatly obliged, Grimsdyke," he went on, "if you would agree to accompany me to New York as my assistant."

I stared at him. "Who, sir? Me, sir?"

"There is always a plague of paper work at these affairs, and your ability with the pen would be useful."

"But I don't know the first thing about executives' health," I pointed out.

"My dear feller, it is only necessary to tell them to skip lunch and walk to the station. If they wish us to travel three thousand miles to do so, that is entirely their affair. Your expenses would be paid, of course. First class."

Naturally, I accepted on the spot. We Grimsdykes are always ready for a free ride anywhere, even if it's only the Woolwich Ferry.

"Excellent. I should moreover appreciate some company, never having been to New York before." Sir Lancelot hesitated at the front door. "I have, in fact, never been abroad before at all."

This was another surprise. Sir Lancelot was the sort of man who gave the impression he had been everywhere except the top of Everest.

"Indeed," he corrected himself, "I did, as a young house surgeon, take a day excursion to Boulogne. But something I ate disagreed with me so violently I have never felt inclined to leave our shores since. We start on Monday fortnight, for three weeks. Now I must just take my afternoon prowl through the bedrooms. I am not at all certain that wretch Quellsby isn't harboring a bar of milk chocolate."

Chapter Three

I should have twigged from the beginning that a trip with Sir Lancelot to New York would be likely to end in a frightful rumpus. Come to think of it, a trip with Sir Lancelot to Elysium would be likely to end in a frightful rumpus, too.

Before we left London Airport he'd lost his hat and his passport, he made a scene on the plane because he couldn't get a glass of hot milk and a digestive biscuit, then he swallowed a handful of barbiturates and snored in my ear all the flight. It took two stewardesses with the ice bucket to wake him up as we landed at Idlewild Airport in New York, just as it was getting dark and Manhattan was putting on its evening diamonds. Dr. Archbold himself was waiting to meet us and turned out to be an amiable quiet little cove in rimless glasses, looking exactly as he did on the cover of *Time*—heart specialists in America, of course, enjoying much the same status as movie stars and top baseball players.

"Very decent of you, coming all this way to greet me, Archbold," began Sir Lancelot, still yawning.

"Gee, it's no bother at all." He led us toward his air-conditioned Cadillac. "I just flew in with my private jet from examining an oil man in Texas."

In the car was Dr. Archbold's secretary, who had blue hair and looked as though she'd just been unwrapped from cellophane. The colored chap at the wheel started driving toward

New York, and I settled back while Dr. Archbold very civilly pointed out the objects of interest on the way.

There's an odd thing about New York. Even though you've never been further west before than Ilfracombe, as soon as you hit the place you suffer what the neurologists call the *déjà-vu* phenomenon—that old I-have-been-here-before feeling. You're perfectly at home among the apparently topless towers and the apparently endless avenues, the advertisements in Times Square that shoot real smoke rings and real waterfalls in the direction of the passers-by, the cars the size of billiard tables, and the police sirens like banshees with some irritating skin complaint. It's all just like the films, in fact. And that's not to mention the hot dogs and Coca-Cola, and the drug stores that stay open all day and all night and sell everything from brassieres to breakfast.

And there's another thing about New York. It's a terrific place, of course, but it seems to have got stuck sometime in a state of confusion that makes dear old London look like a rainy early closing day in Stow-on-the-Wold. As I should have spotted from the start, this left Sir Lancelot like some elderly gentleman trying to play croquet in an earthquake.

"Pardon me," apologized Dr. Archbold, a buzz sounding from his armrest as the car reached our hotel in the middle of Manhattan, where the traffic gets so jammed it looks as though they'll have to send for men with crowbars to get it unstuck again. He picked up a telephone. "Dr. Archbold here . . . yeah . . . well, I guess I can be right over, if I phone my office."

"I'll get your office on the other line, Doctor," said the secretary, picking up a telephone from her own armrest.

"Good gracious me," murmured Sir Lancelot.

Medicine, of course, is now fully mechanized in America, like pretty well everything else there except sex, and some people don't put that past IBM in the near future.

"It's too bad," apologized Dr. Archbold, putting down the

instrument. "I guess I'll have to be mighty inhospitable and leave you at your hotel. I've got to go right out and examine a banker in Boston. I'll take the private helicopter," he added to the secretary.

"Good gracious me," murmured Sir Lancelot.

Dr. Archbold stepped back into the air-conditioned Cadillac. Sir Lancelot and I stepped into the express elevator, which shot up ninety-six stories as though making for Venus and stopped like a butterfly alighting on a rose petal.

"I take a pot of China tea and a digestive biscuit at seven-thirty in the mornings," declared the surgeon to a youth in buttons bringing up our luggage.

"Well, I guess there ain't no law against it, Pop," replied the bellboy cheerfully. "For me, I take a Seven-Up and a cookie."

"The servitors here are pretty chummy, sir," I explained quickly while Sir Lancelot's face went through the colors at the lower end of the spectrum. "It's in the great tradition of American equality. Also, most of them earn about as much as a Harley Street surgeon at home."

Sir Lancelot then carried on because the television set in his room was larger than the bed, and I was glad enough to get away from the old boy to my own apartment at the far end of the corridor. But I'd hardly time to unpack my toothbrush before the house telephone rang, with Sir Lancelot on the wire.

"Grimsdyke, I do not want to cause unnecessary alarm, nor do I wish to precipitate panic among the guests, but I feel we should take some elementary precautions because the hotel is on fire."

"On fire, sir?"

"I thought I made myself perfectly plain—"

"Of course, sir." I gave a nervous glance in the direction of the street. "But where exactly happen to be the smoke and flames, and the other usual things, sir?"

"The conflagration itself is still no doubt undiscovered. But the heat of the blaze has already reached the upper limits of human endurance."

"Perhaps I'd better come round, sir," I suggested quickly.

Sir Lancelot had turned on the air conditioner to maximum midwinter heat, while trying to make the thing emit the radio news bulletin. I reset the knobs for him, but either I mixed them up or Sir Lancelot couldn't resist fiddling with the works, because when he called me back ten minutes later the room was so cold he was starting to ice up round the beard.

"Grimsdyke, I think I could do with a drink," he announced, blowing on his hands.

"Just the thing for restoring the body temperature, I'm sure, sir," I agreed.

Even the drink didn't cheer him up. New York may be the brightest spot in the world, but all its bars are dim, guilty little places, staffed by superannuated warders from Alcatraz. I suppose it's because New Yorkers never bred the prohibition business out of their constitutions. Not for your Madison Avenue chap a leisurely pint with a game of darts and a chat about the crops. He likes to slink in, sink one, and slink out again, regarding drinking as one of those necessary but rather distasteful regular activities, like paring down a painful corn.

"Scotch whiskey should never be consumed at a temperature lower than a Scottish stream," growled the surgeon, as the Alcatraz chap touched the button of a machine that started voiding ice cubes like a frozen chicken in good form.

No New Yorker has tasted a drink in his life, of course, all refreshments being served cold enough immediately to paralyze the taste buds, and the dry martinis arriving at the temperature of liquid oxygen. After that, Sir Lancelot complained about the soft music they pipe everywhere, even in the Gents', and ended up by demanding who this Mr. Rheingold was, whose daughter seemed to be so popular.

I managed to get the old boy through dinner, in a restaurant with a menu the size of a newspaper, which served baked potatoes the size of bolsters and steaks you couldn't finish unless you'd just spent fourteen days adrift in an open boat.

"Good gracious me," murmured Sir Lancelot, when the waiter asked if he'd like to finish off with angel food as his mother made it, then he complained about the bill and the coffee and I began to see that nursing Sir Lancelot through the complexities of New York life was going to be like driving a Model T Ford up and down Broadway.

Chapter Four

～

Early next day I went to collect Sir Lancelot for the conference and found him in a prickly mood in his braces.

"Good morning, sir," I greeted the old boy brightly. "According to the telly, it's going to be a nice hot day by courtesy of Bubblo Soap."

He grunted.

"I trust you slept well, sir, on your Pompadour Beautylaze Couch?"

"Archbold," muttered the surgeon, "who had spent the night flying out to examine a meat packer in Chicago, insisted on discussing the conference agenda over what he described as a 'working breakfast.' To my mind, discussing anything whatever over breakfast is perfectly abnormal. Breakfast is not a meal. It is another of those intimate morning rites necessary to equip one for the day."

Being one who likes to take a bit of a run at the day myself, I sympathized with him.

"I'm afraid our American chums just feel frustrated they can't invent a twenty-five-hour day, sir," I observed. "I hope the breakfast was a decent one?"

Sir Lancelot shrugged his shoulders. "I ordered from the menu some Sunbasked Crushed Vitamin-Chocked Oklahoma Wheat Ears and a Piping Hot Farm-Fresh Present From a Happy Hen. I got a plate of cereal and a boiled egg."

I noticed from his tray the management had tried to make up for this by adding a colored paper cap with *Good Morning, Folks!* written on it, a folder of matches with a girl suffering from mammary hypertrophy on the cover, a sheet of black-edged paper headed *Your Sixty-second Sermon for Today*, and a plastic box done up with ribbons containing a complimentary pink carnation for the buttonhole.

"No gentleman," ended Sir Lancelot sadly, "would, of course, ever contemplate wearing in his buttonhole anything but a *red* carnation."

We slipped down the express elevator to the street, and pretty cozy it was out there, too, particularly as in America, where they do everything properly, they don't only have heat but they have humidity as well. We picked up a cab, the driver put us square on the international situation, and we arrived at the conference in the Liberty Room of the Washington-Herxheimer Hotel.

Early in the proceedings I began to suffer from a chilly feeling that had nothing to do with the air conditioning.

I'm much in favor of medical conferences, as long as they're properly organized. At a medical conference in England they naturally always provide a hall for a few enthusiasts to hear another one rambling away over some cracked lantern slides shown upside down. The rest of the doctors take the chance to clear off and play golf, or to go on the toot with other doctors out of sight of their patients.

But when American doctors hold a conference, they jolly well confer. I was banking on everyone gently drifting away once Archbold had raised the tapes with his presidential address, so I could pass a happy three weeks seeing the sights of New York, such as Jack Dempsey's Bar and the burlesque shows I'd read about in Damon Runyon. But those enthusiastic chaps went hammering at the door of knowledge from eight in the morning till six at night, with an hour off at noon for waffle-burgers and Coca-Cola. And anyone mounting the rostrum with a folder of notes slimmer than the Manhattan telephone directory was clearly thought to be betraying the great traditions of American oratory.

"Thank you, Grimsdyke, for kicking me on the ankle when I started to snore," mentioned Sir Lancelot, when we were released at the end of the day.

"Not a bit, sir. Always glad to avert an international incident."

"I fear I must have been sadly wrong over the years," he sighed, "when I held at St. Swithin's that anyone could express all his knowledge of any scientific subject on a post card. Though how an executive or anyone else can possibly ever feel completely healthy in this place is totally beyond me."

He indicated with his umbrella a poster outside the subway announcing that we'd arrived in National Nephrosis Week, while from other posters I gathered the citizens had only just got over National Hemiplegia Week and could look forward after Sunday to a jolly National Schizophrenia Week.

"Our American chums are well up with the clinical articles in the *Reader's Digest*, and regard *Time* as the great healer, sir," I suggested. "They'd never fork out for our dear old British charities with their 'Spare a Copper for the Distressed Gentlefolk' or 'Our Roof is Leaking.'"

"They certainly have an eye for clinical detail. Even in the obituary pages of the newspapers. The New York *Times* this morning quite reminded me in parts of the *Pathologist's Handbook*."

I nodded. "Particularly as the undertakers oil round the margins with cosy invitations to let them lay you out on the never-never. Could make an executive feel pretty nasty over breakfast I should think, particularly on hot mornings with a hangover."

"Odd," mused Sir Lancelot, hailing a cab, "that everyone here should take death so extremely seriously."

But Americans don't pass their days simply looking forward to their absolutely slap-up funeral, any more than we spend ours puffing our churchwardens in our smocks at the doors of our thatched cottages, in between Morris dancing and trying to trace our ancestors. The clouds of oratory were brightened no end by the nightly flashes of hospitality, and after a week even Sir Lancelot started making concessions to the New World, such as drinking Scotch-on-the-rocks and calling Archbold by his Christian name. Though he still wouldn't dress up in white blouse and trousers like Dr. Kildare to visit Archbold's private hospital, saying he refused to go round looking like a ruddy West End hairdresser. For years, of course, he had found it unnecessary to go round looking like anything but Sir Lancelot Spratt.

As for our hosts, they took to calling him "Lance" and asking him all about our National Health Service, even though they did infer that anyone walking about with a mouthful of free teeth was undermining the great traditions of Western democracy.

"It is now four o'clock," announced Sir Lancelot, snapping open his watch in the middle of Fifth Avenue on the Saturday afternoon, which was free for sight-seeing. "And I must confess I should much like a peaceful cup of tea."

The old boy had certainly passed a wearying day, what with being answered back by a talking mailbox and trying to find where they hid the trains in Grand Central Station. Particularly as the temperature was so high I fancied the heat was even getting into the martinis.

"If one can obtain such a thing as tea in the tumult of this urban Niagara," he added.

"That looks a quiet little spot over there," I suggested, indicating a neon sign. "The one that's called The Haven of Rest."

"That should suit me perfectly."

I must say, we took to the place as soon as we stepped off the sizzling sidewalk under the striped canopy and pushed through the big plate-glass doors into the soothing air conditioning.

"A very decent small hotel," conceded Sir Lancelot, glancing approvingly round the lobby.

"Just the spot for a long cool beer," I nodded.

The lobby was done in a restful purple, with some well-coiffeured bunches of flowers standing agreeably in the corners. There was piped music, naturally, but instead of *Top Hat* and *South Pacific* it was soft and gentle stuff played quietly on the organ. Best of all, there seemed absolutely no one about, making a change from our own hotel lobby, which was bags and bustle all round the clock.

"Not much sign of life," I remarked. "I suppose the cafeteria's on the roof."

"Do you know, Grimsdyke," announced Sir Lancelot suddenly, "I've more than half a mind to move my quarters here for the rest of the conference. You stay where you are, of course. This is far too quiet for you. But it will suit myself absolutely down to the ground."

At that moment a purple door marked "Reception" opened, emitting a thin pale chap with gray hair, wearing the usual black jacket and striped trousers.

"Good afternoon, gentlemen," said the chap, in a quiet respectful voice that seemed to please Sir Lancelot no end. "I am Mr. Samboys, the manager here. May I ask whom you have called to see?"

"We haven't called to see anyone," I told him.

"Ah, no," murmured the manager.

"As a matter of fact," went on Sir Lancelot, "I wondered if you happened to have a room available."

Mr. Samboys let fall a sigh.

"I'm real sorry, sir, but at this moment all our rooms are occupied."

"I only want a single room," added Sir Lancelot. "Not a double."

The manager looked a bit worried at this, but apologized, "We're mighty busy this time of the year, sir. I guess it's the sudden heat."

"Quite," nodded the surgeon. "Had I any acquaintances visiting New York just now, I should do my utmost to get them into one of your cool rooms. I have formed an excellent impression of the establishment."

Mr. Samboys bowed.

"I suppose I couldn't book a room for later?"

The manager gave a smile and a quick rub of the hands.

"Sure you can, sir. We always advise folks to think ahead."

"Naturally."

"Who would the room be for, sir?"

Sir Lancelot frowned slightly. "For myself, of course. I suppose you can give me a definite date? I shall be needing it quite soon."

Mr. Samboys' smile sagged a bit in the middle.

"Quite soon, sir?"

"Exactly," Sir Lancelot told him briskly. "In the next day or two at the latest. Indeed, I am quite ready to move in now."

"My deepest condolences," muttered the manager.

"I say," I chipped in, feeling pretty thirsty. "Do you think you could fix me up with a beer?"

The manager's jaw unhinged rather more. "Fix you up with a bier? What, right now?"

"Yes, of course. Where's the bar?"

"Say," exclaimed Mr. Samboys. "Do you guys know where you are?"

"Damnation, man," exploded Sir Lancelot. "This is the Haven of Rest Hotel—"

"It's the Haven of Rest Funeral Parlor, that's what," said the manager, staring a bit.

"Grimsdyke!" hissed Sir Lancelot.

"Sorry," I apologized. "Wrong number."

"Hey, wait a minute!" As we made for the door, Mr. Samboys replaced his smile and did a quick handwash. "You gentlemen have got to think of the future. Yes, sir! And our terms are mighty moderate. We've buried five generations right here in New York City. We have a fine name for consideration of the bereaved ones' feelings, particularly financial. We have five stories of magnificently appointed air-conditioned apartments—"

Sir Lancelot grabbed the door handle.

"Not today," I told the chap.

"But say, listen. We do a mighty fine embalming job on easy terms." Mr. Samboys gave a little laugh. "Die now, pay later, you know."

"No thank you!" roared Sir Lancelot.

"My friend here," I explained to Mr. Samboys, "already has his do-it-yourself kit."

We stepped onto the roasting sidewalk.

"Embarrassing," muttered Sir Lancelot. "Damnably embarrassing."

There's one thing, sir," I said consolingly. "At least you've tried the only digs in New York where they don't advertise all the rooms with television."

Chapter Five

〜

It was at three the following morning that my bedside telephone rang.

"Grimsdyke? Spratt here."

"Oh, hello, Sir Lancelot." I was naturally rather fuddled at that hour. "Surely you're not still in the Conference for Extending Executives' Existence?"

"I am not in any ruddy conference. I am in jail."

"You're in *what*, sir?"

"In jail, you fool! Can't you hear me?"

"Yes, yes, of course, sir."

After the Haven of Rest, I felt used to surprising things happening in New York at a rate that made *Alice in Wonderland* read like Mrs. Beeton's cooking book. But I was pretty startled to learn that the place had now got the Emeritus Senior Surgeon of St. Swithin's Hospital incarcerated in the nick.

"Shall—shall I send for the British Ambassador, sir?"

"I very much doubt if His Excellency would be roused from his slumbers to take a personal hand in the crisis. You will kindly come yourself with the utmost dispatch and get me out."

"Get you out, sir?"

"Will you stop making those irritating bleating noises on the end of the line, man?"

The old boy was understandably a bit short-tempered.

"I mean, where are you in, sir?"

"I am at this moment in the corner of an extremely uncomfortable and overheated room, in the company of a large number of highly unprepossessing persons, whose appearance of villainy is to my mind exceeded by that of the police officers standing among us with loaded firearms."

"Good lord, sir."

"You will find me in a police station at the corner of Sixty-seventh Street and Lexington Avenue, on what they call the East Side. Be good enough to leave your bed instantly."

"Yes, of course, sir."

"And Grimsdyke—"

"Sir?"

"You will not mention one word of this to a soul."

"No, of course not, sir."

"Thank you. I shall reimburse you the taxi fare."

I switched on the light and reached for my trousers, feeling like a nervous French revolutionary on the morning of July the fourteenth.

"I am not at all sorry to be without an engagement tonight," was the last Sir Lancelot had said to me, hiding a yawn as we sat over a Scotch in the alcoholic grotto earlier. "Archbold asked me to dine, but he had to go out in his private yacht to examine a movie producer arriving on the *Queen Elizabeth*. I fear, anyway, that yesterday's dinner with full symphony orchestra and aquacabaret was rather too much for me. I shall tonight content myself with a light meal in an establishment known, I believe, as the Hamburger Heaven. I am sure, Grimsdyke, you would prefer to be left to your own devices, so I shall not press you to accompany me."

As a matter of fact, I was so exhausted from a week's nannying Sir Lancelot, I nipped into the hotel grill for a Protein-Packed Chunk of Milk-Reared Ram with Man-Sized Marrowbone (a mutton chop), went up to bed, switched on the telly, watched the Late Show, the Late Late Show, and possibly the Early Early Show, and quietly dropped off.

And now I was on my way to the chokey, wondering what sort of crimes Sir Lancelot had been up to before getting himself put inside.

I wondered if he might simply have been mistaken for some leading New York gangster, except that all the leading New York gangsters now are aged about sixteen. Then I reflected it was easy enough to find yourself in jail anywhere these days, what with income tax and the way some people try and cross the road. And the jails in New York are particularly accessible to the general public, some of the less respectable citizens being so unrespectable altogether the police tend to handle any rumpus with arrests all round and a merry sorting out later.

I easily found the police station, which, like all the other amenities of New York at that hour on a Saturday night, was fully open and doing a thriving business—nobody in Manhattan has been to bed for years and years, of course. I stepped past the photographs of chaps the authorities would like a word with, and gingerly approached a tall desk with a cop sitting behind it—a fat, bald, dark fellow, with the expression of having witnessed all the depravities of the world and having got pretty fed up with them, like those pictures of the Emperor Nero.

"Yeah?" said the cop.

"Er—good evening, officer."

"Yeah."

It was a bit difficult knowing where to start.

"My name is Dr. Grimsdyke."

"Yeah?"

The cop had a bit of a chew at his gum.

"I am calling on behalf of the prisoner Spratt."

"Ah, yeah."

The cop brightened up, like the Emperor Nero reaching for his music when he heard the crackle of flames.

"You a psychiatrist?" asked the cop.

"A psychiatrist? No, not actually."

"Because a psychiatrist is what that guy sure needs. Yes, sir. Is he a nut!"

"A bit eccentric, possibly," I agreed. "But quite safe in public."

"See here. The guy first says he's an English lord—"

"An English knight. Like King Arthur's pals on the telly."

"Then the guy says he's a famous English doctor. I don't get it. Don't lords just sit round all day in golden crowns eatin' crumpets?"

Americans sometimes have a hazy idea of life in the English aristocracy, I suppose through all those gin advertisements. But I felt it wasn't the moment to explain the niceties of Debrett, and merely asked:

"What's the—er, charge, officer."

"Ah, yeah."

The cop now looked like the Emperor Nero with a broken string just as the blaze got nicely started.

"The charge is obstructin' a police officer in the execution of his duty and usin' foul language on the sidewalk. Hey, O'Reilly," he directed another cop. "Bring in Spratt."

In a couple of minutes Sir Lancelot appeared through a steel gate leading to the guest accommodation. As I'd expected, a spell in the cooler had only stoked up his emotional temperature. He glared at the Emperor Nero. His beard was quivering like a terrier spotting a postman. He shook with indignation to the very ferrule of his umbrella.

"Extremely good of you to come, Grimsdyke," he snorted. "You will now kindly explain to these constables exactly who I am. Then I might be spared more of this perfectly intolerable

indignity and we might both obtain a little sleep in what remains of the night."

"Why ain't ya carrying ya passport?" demanded the cop.

"Because, my man, I have never in my life found it necessary
to walk about with a piece of paper explaining who I am."

"Ya used foul language on the sidewalk," the cop persisted.

"I certainly did not use foul language on the sidewalk. I have
never used foul language anywhere in my life."

"Ya called the patrolman an insolent pip-squeak." The cop
took out his gum and inspected it sadly, as though it were some
faithful old pet nearing its last legs. "Sounds like mighty foul
language to me."

I began to see what the fuss was about, and pretty worried
it made me, too. You can always try a bit of give and take
with an English rozzer, and no hard feelings. But you have to
go pretty cagily with the New York constabulary, particularly
when you remember they walk about swinging ruddy great
baseball bats, and are so ringed round the middle with revolver
bullets they look in danger of going off on hot afternoons like
a Guy Fawkes' set-piece.

Sir Lancelot slapped the desk with his umbrella. "The con-
stable officiously tried to prevent my crossing the street."

"Yeah. The street sign was signaling 'Don't Walk.' "

"At my age," declared the surgeon, drawing himself up, "I
believe I know how to cross the road."

"Aw, sure," grunted the cop.

America may be the Land of the Free, but they're pretty
hot on the traditional liberty of British subjects to wander
all over the road and chuck themselves under the buses.

"The officer was tryin' to stop ya walking alone in Central
Park," the cop ended wearily.

"And why not, pray?" Sir Lancelot glared. "I much favor a
stroll in the park before I turn in."

"Brother! You stroll in Central Park at night, and the only place you'll turn into will be the mortician's."

I didn't know what to say. As pointed out in *The New Yorker*, our American chums are terribly clever chaps who will soon be walking about on the outer planets, but they haven't yet fixed things so they can wander through Central Park after nightfall without risking, from those less respectable citizens, a process technically known as "a mugging."

"I wish to see your superior officer," commanded Sir Lancelot.

"I guess I'm the superior officer here."

"I demand to be released instantly."

"O'Reilly," said the cop, with the air of the Emperor Nero tiring of the gladiators and anxious to turn to the Christians and lions, "take this guy down to the psychopathic cell."

"Look here," I pitched in, now thoroughly alarmed, "you can't do a thing like that."

"Yeah? Who says so?"

"I do," I told him stoutly.

"O'Reilly—take that guy down to the nut cage, too."

"I mean, officer." I corrected myself. "There has possibly been some slight misunderstanding—"

"Get movin'," growled O'Reilly, who seemed about eight feet tall and with enough armament to stop a tank.

"Here, just a minute—"

"Git movin', I sez."

I suppose we should both have been shipped out to Sing-Sing in strait jackets if the air-conditioned Cadillac hadn't drawn up and Dr. Archbold shot in.

"Good God, what's *he* doing here?" exclaimed Sir Lancelot.

I let out a ruddy great sigh.

"I took the liberty, sir, of putting through a call to Dr. Archbold's apartment from the hotel."

Sir Lancelot turned his glare on me. "You did *what?* In defiance of my strict and explicit instructions—"

"Very sorry, sir."

"How *dare* you, Grimsdyke!"

"Beg your pardon, sir."

"You and I will most certainly have a word about this in the morning. Most certainly! What the world is coming to I really don't know. Nobody seems to take the slightest notice of me any more."

And there, I felt, the old boy had put his finger on the wound.

Dr. Archbold, who couldn't have made more impression if he'd been the President himself, quickly sorted everything out and in a few minutes was wafting us away in the air-conditioned Cadillac.

"You know, Lancelot, I'm mighty sorry a mistake like that happened," our host tried to console him.

Sir Lancelot grunted.

"New York is a confusing city. Yes, sir," he reflected. "I guess you need to relax. Say, how about taking my Boeing down to my ranch in Colorado tomorrow?"

"Kind of you, Archbold, but I really don't think—"

"I guess you'll find it just like home down there. I got a butler from Buckingham Palace. You can take it easy, just mooching around in one of the helicopters."

"But the conference—" objected Sir Lancelot.

"Oh, we can put that on my private television circuit." Archbold suddenly looked worried. "I guess you won't mind if it's not in color, huh?"

"Good gracious me," muttered Sir Lancelot. "Goodness gracious me."

Chapter Six

When I knocked on Sir Lancelot's door in the morning, I found him in his braces finishing his Bonnie Scotland Body-Builder and Orb of Florida Sunshine (porridge and grapefruit).

"Grimsdyke," he greeted me somberly, "I feel I have experienced a rather bad dream."

"Don't worry, sir." I tried to cheer him up. "The story will never get home to St. Swithin's. Admittedly, I broke security with chum Archbold, but usually I am the very soul of discretion."

"You are very far from it," he said wearily, "though I think I can trust you to keep your mouth shut on this occasion. Your better self, at least, will feel indebted to me for its fare."

I noticed his suitcase was packed.

"When are you off to Colorado, sir?"

"I am not."

"Not, sir?"

"Unfortunately, a cable recalls me to see an important case in London."

"Oh, really? What a dashed shame. When did it arrive?"

"The cable will be arriving during the morning, possibly before my departure. You will kindly show it to Archbold with appropriate apologies, and attend the remainder of the conference yourself." Sir Lancelot reflectively took a bite of his Sizzling Hot Buttered Staff of Life. "I fear, Grimsdyke, that I have, all considered, had rather too much of executives' health."

"And that's why I'm flying back alone," I explained to Lucy Squiffington, after making the story last a good slice of the Atlantic.

"But you poor dear! New York certainly lived up to its reputation as one of the world's most exciting cities."

"Oh, things quieted down a good deal once I got Sir Lancelot airborne. After that, I used to clock in at the conference in the morning, then slip down the freight elevator and see all those sights of New York I mentioned."

"Including the burlesque?" Lucy smiled.

"No, they've shut that down now. I went to the United Nations instead."

The vicar's daughter interrupted to ask if we held British passports, rather inferring it was rotten luck if we didn't.

"But quite apart from New York, Lucy," I ventured, "the whole trip was worth it just to run into you once more."

She switched on the eyes again. "Now, isn't that sweet of you, Gaston?"

"I've often wished I'd had the sense at Whortleton to ask for your phone number."

She laughed.

"Look here," I persevered. "It seems a shocking pity our just parting for good and all once the airline ticket runs out. I mean, couldn't we have a little drink in town some evening? Just for old times' sake."

"But Gaston, of course. I'd love to."

"I say, would you really?" I suddenly felt all warm inside, as though I'd swallowed a sunset. "Here's my address and phone number." I scribbled on a bit of the waterproof brown-paper bag they tuck into the seat in front. "I've got a little mews flat down in Chelsea."

"That sounds terribly romantic."

"Not really. It's only a converted horses' larder."

"Fasten your seat belts and no smoking," announced the vicar's daughter over the intercom. "We hope you have had a pleasant flight."

Pleasant flight? I thought. As far as I was concerned I could happily have gone on flying right round the world.

There's nothing like an airport for bringing you down to earth. Apart from the freezing drizzle howling across the tarmac, more bossy girls in uniform, and the Customs men eyeing you as though you were Blackbeard the Pirate after a decent shave, it was eight o'clock in the morning all round and still only 3 A.M. inside me. And that wasn't to mention the effect of all those free martinis wearing off.

I lost Lucy Squiffington in the Customs hall, and I must say I wasn't really sorry. I caught sight of her through the crowd outside climbing into a plum-colored Rolls with chauffeur to match, and it struck me what a cloud-cuckoo-land I'd been living in. As I remembered, Pa Squiffington owned half a bank, and though I suppose the family couldn't just drop in and fill up their wallets as necessary, a girl like Lucy must have attracted the chaps like a picnic attracts wasps. With elegant coves bearing titles and little moustaches hanging round her throughout London and the Home Counties, what could she see in seedy old Grimsdyke, in his rumpled suit and his nylon shirt he'd forgotten to wash the night before? Once she had her feet on the ground, the poor girl must have felt like Miranda when Caliban started getting uppish. I gave a bit of a sigh. Come to think of it, there's nothing in the world quite so egalitarian as first-class travel.

I climbed onto the airport bus, keen to get home for shave and a bath. Besides, I had to telephone my fiancée.

Chapter Seven

~

"Hello?" I said over the line. "Is that the Home for Delinquent Females?"

"Delinquent females speaking."

"Do you think you could get Miss Anemone for me?"

"Miss Anemone? Just one moment, please."

I was standing in the corner of my horses' larder, holding the telephone and turning over the pages of the daily paper—a poor anemic little thing after the New York *Times*, which is liable to suffocate anyone reading it in bed, and on Sundays comes in handy if the family wants to go out camping.

"Hello?" Anemone's nice voice came on the wire.

"Hello, Nenny. Here's Gaston, back in circulation."

"Why, Gaston! And how was Cheltenham?"

"Cheltenham was fine, thanks. Very bracing."

"I'm so glad," she said nicely. "What was the weather like?"

"Oh, sort of mixed."

"And how's your grandmother?"

"The old dear's in cracking form. Apart from her usual back, of course."

"You might have rung me up just once, Gaston," Anemone chided me, though of course in a nice way.

"But I told you, old girl, grandma won't have a phone. She says it attracts the lightning in thunderstorms."

"Yes, but . . . well, you could have used a public telephone, couldn't you, Gaston?"

Odd, I'd never thought of that.

"Oh, but I did. Unfortunately, I hadn't the right change. You'd be surprised what a terribly complicated combination of sixpences and shillings you need to get through to you in the country."

There was a bit of a pause.

"You're certain you still want to come down to the seaside with us?" Anemone went on, not seeming particularly sympathetic about the sixpences.

"Sure I do, baby. It's going to be swell."

"Good heavens, Gaston! Since when have you taken to using American expressions?"

"That's the films. I went to a frightful lot of films in Cheltenham. Nothing else to do."

"Mummy says she hopes you weren't bored."

"That's very decent of her. Actually, the grandma's no end of a conversationalist for her age."

"She means she hopes you weren't so bored you went out drinking."

"Not so much as a pint of good old English beer has passed my lips."

Remarkable how smug you can feel when you're actually telling the truth.

"Must ring off," I apologized. "The place is thick with threads I've got to pick up now I'm back in town."

"But Gaston, you sound as though you've been to the other side of the earth."

"That's the feeling you get in Cheltenham. Bye-bye, Nenny. See you soon."

"'Bye, Gaston."

I gave the telephone a subconscious wipe with my sleeve, as though I'd infected it with something nasty. It was a pretty

rotten way to behave toward a nice girl like Anemone. I
sighed deeply. Like drowning kittens or fiddling your income
tax, it was regrettable but it couldn't be avoided.

And Anemone really *was* a nice girl. Everyone she met said
so.

"What a nice girl, Dame Hilda Parkhouse's daughter," observed my older cousin Miles, calling at my flat the morning
after introducing the pair of us during a party at his own
house in Kensington.

"Yes, a very nice girl," I agreed.

Which was odd, our ideas on women usually differing as
much as Michelangelo's from Epstein's.

"I fancy Dame Hilda was pleased to notice you so attentive
to the young lady," remarked Miles, with one of those wintery
smiles of his.

"Oh, was I?"

I'd simply been passing Anemone the sausages on sticks and
the little fishy things. Though I suppose one does become rather
attentive toward unaccompanied blondes one finds at parties,
even on Miles's fruit cup.

"Dame Hilda," continued Miles, taking another of his smiles
from the deep freeze, "thought you a charming young man."

"Really? Very decent of her."

"I did not, of course, say anything to disillusion her. I should
prefer Dame Hilda to imagine that our family flock presented
a uniformly white appearance."

That remark was typical of Miles. He was a chap whose one
regret at the breakup of the British Empire was it leaving us
short of uncomfortable colonies to ship people like me to.

"Dame Hilda is, of course, a most important figure in our
national life," my cousin went on, as I let the slur pass like
a bad ball outside the off stump. "As a personal friend of the
Prime Minister, I believe she could procure even me a safe seat

in Parliament any time she felt inclined. 'Miles Grimsdyke, M.P.' That would be a joke, wouldn't it? Eh? Ha, ha!"

"Ha, ha," I said.

"Or even a life peerage, what? Ha, ha, ha!"

"Ha, ha, ha," I said.

"Not to mention her being a lifelong confidante of Lady Spratt. I fancy she could bring pressure on Sir Lancelot to find even you a respectable position in the National Health Service. Ha, ha, ha, ha!"

"Ha," I said.

Miles had become buddies with Dame Hilda when they'd both sat on the Royal Commission to Inquire into the State of Public Morality. My cousin was a severe little chap with a bristly moustache, whom the family mentioned in the same breath as myself only when pointing out how interesting the variations were in the heredity of intelligence. He was not only the youngest surgeon on the consultant staff of St. Swithin's Hospital, but also a great one for blocking up our sociological rat holes, and I fancy saw himself going down in the history books as the fellow who finally put the country right by stopping everyone buying a packet of fags after eight o'clock or going to watch Shakespeare on Sundays.

As for Dame Hilda, she was the well-known penologist you kept seeing on the telly, who busied herself sorting out the odd fish thrown up by the crime waves. At the time of the party Miles and Dame Hilda were having no end of fun together going round the prisons, trying to decide for the government if chaps who sandbagged old ladies should be told they were naughty boys and not to do it again, or sent across to the Tower and given a go on the rack.

But I should never have become engaged to Anemone, or even seen her again, if it hadn't been for a series of amazing coincidences.

A couple of evenings after the party Miles telephoned to say

a patient whose stomach he'd removed had sent him a couple of
seats for the latest musical, but as he had an emergency appendix in St. Swithin's perhaps I could take Anemone instead?

"Anemone so rarely enjoys the lighter amusements of London," he explained over the line. "She's such a nice girl, so
devoted to helping her mother with the delinquent females of
Yorkshire."

I quite enjoyed the musical, and Anemone was a perfectly
nice companion. She was a girl with that fair, healthy, weather-
proof sort of beauty, which is understandably so popular in
England. Admittedly, she went about looking like a badly furled
umbrella, but she didn't talk too much and she laughed at all
my jokes, though I only told her the nice ones, of course.

Now, the odd thing was, three days later Miles rang to say
he'd a couple of tickets for the new comedy from a patient
whose gall bladder he'd removed, but he'd been called to St.
Swithin's to do an emergency splenectomy. It was a nice little
comedy and Anemone and I laughed no end, and I could really
sympathize with poor Miles's rotten luck when the very next
evening he telephoned to say he'd got a couple of stalls for the
Old Vic from a patient whose warts he'd removed, but couldn't
go because of an emergency meeting of the Hospital committee.

The Old Vic was fine, all blood and blank verse, though
when Miles appeared himself the next morning waving a
couple of seats for the latest ice show from someone he'd cured
of chronic chilblains, he found me sitting up in bed shivering.

"It's only my share of the flu epidemic," I snuffled. "I must
have picked it up in all those crowded theaters. I can cure it in
a jiffy with a bottle of whiskey and a hat."

"And how do you intend to do that, pray?"

"Go to bed, put the hat on the bedpost, and drink the whiskey
till the hat moves."

"You must not take influenza lightly, Gaston." Miles, being
a consultant, couldn't treat any sort of illness without making

a frightful fuss about it. "You may quite easily develop a staphylococcal pneumonia."

He produced his stethoscope.

"Alcohol is out of the question, of course," he announced, pocketing my cigarettes for good measure. "And naturally you will need nursing. I will send someone round twice a day to rub your back."

He left me staring at the low ceiling with that frightful filleted feeling you get with flu. Then Anemone suddenly appeared, loaded with magazines, fruit, and Gee's linctus.

"Miles couldn't get anyone at the nursing bureau," she explained with a nice smile. "So Mummy suggested I volunteered instead."

"But dash it!" I sneezed back at her. "That'll completely ruin your stay in London."

"I shall enjoy it, Gaston."

She started to smooth my pillow. Her face took on a saintly look, like the girls in the disinfectant advertisements.

"I always wanted to take up nursing," she continued softly, "except that some of the things you have to do aren't very nice. Now where can I make you some barley water?"

Anemone came every morning and left at teatime—naturally, there was nothing whatever about the arrangements you could possibly think as not quite nice. I must say she cheered me up no end, even when the terrible influenzal depression crept up, until you reach the stage when you stop thinking even the political speeches in the newspapers are funny. Then one afternoon I suddenly realized I was wondering where I'd hidden my spare cigarettes, and Anemone brought me my first lightly boiled egg, and I found I was asking her to marry me.

Chapter Eight

∿

"I am absolutely delighted," declared Miles, appearing early the next morning to discover me alone in my dressing gown. "And Dame Hilda's absolutely delighted, too."

"Glad to be spreading so much happiness this beastly foggy weather." I sneezed modestly.

"Anemone is not only such a nice girl, but her experience as a social worker will have an invaluable effect on you. I only hope and pray, Gaston—as your cousin you must occasionally allow me a certain frankness—"

"Always very refreshing, I assure you."

"I pray Anemone will bring you to your senses and restore you to the proper paths of medicine. Instead of frittering away your life ever since publishing that frivolous novel of yours. You have not only found a wife, Gaston. With her you will find your soul."

Decent of him, except his tone gave the impression a soul like mine hadn't much market value.

"Both the delights and duties of married life are, I fear, shabbily regarded in this sinful age," mentioned Miles, putting a thermometer under my tongue. He went on to point out how he himself at home was a combination of Queen Victoria's Prince Albert and the Swiss Family's Mr. Robinson. "Now that young Bartholomew has arrived to share with Connie and my-self our little nest—"

"Talking of little nests," I remarked, removing the thermometer, "I shall be needing a bit of the old grandpa's cash you've been holding in trust for me."

"Rest assured, Gaston," said Miles, putting it in again, "that I shall promptly make over your portion of the estate on your marriage."

"But now we're pretty well ordering the cake," I indicated, taking out the thermometer, "I expect you'd like to let me have a little on account."

"I shall unobtrusively slip the check into the tail pocket of your morning coat in the vestry," said Miles, popping the thermometer back. "Just as soon as you have signed the register. Ninety-eight point four," he added. "You may go out."

I felt sorry for old Miles with that nasty suspicious mind of his. In fact, I had never been engaged before—admittedly, on occasion I might possibly have been party to some perfectly informal arrangement—but once Anemone and I had plighted our troth in *The Times* I was solidly determined to do the right thing by her. After all, we Grimsdykes have our honor, even if it does need a bit of breathing on and polishing up from time to time. When we pledge our heart—or even our grandpa's old pocket watch—we are perfectly sincere about it. Particularly, I kept reminding myself, as I'd picked such a nice girl as Anemone.

"When, my children," asked Dame Hilda over the teacups, during the weekend I spent with the delinquent females before slipping off to New York, "are you thinking of naming the happy day?"

"Ah, yes. The happy day," I observed.

"Mind you," Dame Hilda went on, "I am not saying that you should in any way rush matters."

"No, of course not."

"In my work I see far too many tragedies from young people rushing blindly into marriage."

"Very tragic, yes," I said, exchanging a nod of agreement across the table with Anemone.

"I do indeed often feel we have swung too far from the Victorian concept of long engagements," reflected her mother.

"Jolly wise birds, the Victorians."

"But you have," murmured Dame Hilda, passing the Madeira cake, "now been engaged over eighteen months."

"Oh, really?" I looked surprised. "Time does fly, doesn't it?"

"Indeed, it does."

Dame Hilda paused to pour the tea. She was a handsome woman, like one of those old-fashioned opera singers, well nourished on bites of managers and conductors. If I'd been a delinquent female, she'd have scared the daylights out of me.

"I read in a magazine the other day the Bourbon kings were engaged to their future queens for years and years," I remarked, feeling she might be interested.

"They were, of course, betrothed in early infancy," returned Dame Hilda, rather distantly. "However, I'm sure you both know your own minds."

Anemone herself was far too nice to enter a delicate conversation like this, but she now chipped in with:

"Mummy, isn't it smashing—Gaston says he can come on our fortnight at Whortleton-on-Sea after all."

Dame Hilda's eyes lit up.

"So you managed to free yourself from all those professional entanglements?"

"Been working at it like a Houdini."

"I'm sure a rest by the sea will do you the world of good. You know Whortleton already, I believe?"

I nodded. "Though I haven't had a dip in the briny there for years and years. And I've probably quite lost my touch with the local shrimps."

"We always stay in that charming hotel overlooking the prom. Anemone and myself share a room, and now I shall ask the management to reserve another for you. I'm sure you young people will find plenty there to amuse yourselves. Perhaps you remember, there is the Aquarium and the Floral Clock, and in the evenings an excellent pierrot show on the pier and bingo in the Winter Gardens." Dame Hilda gave a smile. "I fancy, Gaston, you won't leave Whortleton without definitely fixing your wedding day. Not after I've had a fortnight's work on you—I mean, not after a fortnight of its romantic charm has worked on you. Do have one of these little pink cakes. You'd never imagine the girl who made them cut up her baby brother."

Anemone and myself then went out for a nice game of tennis (she knew some very nice people in the local tennis club). But I must say I bashed the ball over the net with the faint feeling that Dame Hilda sometimes tried to organize my life, rather. Come to think of it, I recalled, watching Anemone's nice service, ever since I'd been engaged Dame Hilda had treated me as though I were on the strength of her delinquent females. There'd been no end of a row that winter, just because I'd slipped over to Paris with some of the chaps from St. Swithin's for the rugby International. It seemed Dame Hilda somehow disliked my escaping from the respectable network of British Railways, so I didn't go out of my way to mention I was making for New York.

I hated lying to a nice girl like Anemone, of course. Even when there was a jolly good chance of my never being found out. Now I reflected that two weeks of looking at Dame Hilda in a swimsuit was going to be hell, and that wasn't to mention those pierrots, but if I'd have backed out of their holiday as well, when I was dead and opened they'd have found "Whortleton" written on my heart.

All this didn't stop me feeling a frightful cad as I put down the telephone after ringing Anemone the morning of my return from New York. I got into the bath deciding that my conduct

certainly wasn't that expected of a man shortly coming up to
his second engagement anniversary. Saying you're in Cheltenham when you're really in America might be passed off as a
mere slip of geography. But making dates with beautiful girls
in airplanes wasn't at all the same thing, even if you'd once
been sick with them behind the same bathing hut. Odd, I mused,
how my sex life over the years had centered round the Whortleton seashore, like the gastropoda. I turned off the hot tap with
my toe, making the decision of Sydney Carton under similar
circumstances. If by any chance Lucy should happen to telephone, I would merely plead an urgent engagement in Yorkshire and send her a slice of wedding cake.

The telephone rang.

"Hello?" I said, dripping a good deal on the carpet.

"Gaston?"

"Why, hello, Lucy."

"I hope it's not inconvenient for me to ring?"

"Inconvenient? Good lord, no. Not in the slightest."

"I wanted to say how sorry I was missing you at the airport.
I was going to offer you a lift into town in my car."

"That Customs man was a bit foxed over the tariff on models
of the Empire State Building, with snowstorm."

"But that isn't all. I got home to find George had turned up.
He's in a terrible state."

"I'd suggest a cup of black coffee and an aspirin for a
start—"

"I mean, the poor dear's in an awful state of nerves. I'm
sure his work is getting far too much for him, Gaston. He
really ought to see a doctor, but Mummy's in St. Tropez and
Daddy's organizing a new branch of the bank in Karachi, and
of course George won't do a thing I tell him myself. So I
wondered if it would be an awful bore for you to come round
and look at him?"

"Bore? Good gracious, no. Absolutely delighted to have a look at George any time."

After all, meeting beautiful girls on the quiet for drinks was one thing. But a professional visit to the family was quite another.

"Gaston, you're a dear, and I'll never be able to tell you how grateful I am. Our flat's in Brook Street, near Claridge's. If you're not too exhausted, after the flight, why not come round this afternoon for a cup of tea?"

I scribbled down the address, climbed back into the bath, soaped myself all over, and sang *"Rule Britannia."*

Chapter Nine

∽

I ran in some more hot water and finished the crossword and my third cigarette, and modestly congratulated myself that life was for once turning over like some well-oiled piece of machinery. I'd enjoyed a jolly good trip to New York incognito, now I'd only an afternoon's work finishing off my report on the conference for Sir Lancelot, then I should have the pleasure of once again meeting my dear old friend Squiffy —and possibly I might bump into that charming younger sister of his at the same time.

I reached out of the bath for my model of the Empire State Building in its little globe, and made a few snowstorms. It's remarkable how contented you can feel soaking in warm water and thinking of nothing. Such a pity the psychiatrists try to spoil it all by insisting it's only our daily attempt to return to the conditions of the womb.

My peace was exploded by a terrific knocking on the front door.

In my horses' larder you can pretty well unlatch the front door from the bath, but I lay under the water like a cagey hippopotamus. As the knocking became even louder it occurred to me the Fire Brigade might be standing rather impatiently on the mat, so I jumped from the bath, slung a towel round my waist, and opened up.

Outside was my cousin Miles, with a suitcase.

"Where the devil have you been?" he demanded crossly. "I was telephoning you almost hourly all yesterday."

"Oh, hello, Miles." I looked surprised. "As a matter of fact I've only just got back from New—Cheltenham."

"Cheltenham? What the hell were you doing in Cheltenham?"

"I was looking up our old grandma."

Miles frowned. "Peculiar. When she saw me about her back in Harley Street the other week she didn't mention you were paying a visit."

"Very forgetful these old folk, you know. Senile degeneration of the arteries—"

"Yes, yes, yes," snapped Miles.

He came in, chucked down his suitcase, and sat heavily on my divan.

My cousin stared at the floor for some moments in silence. But from the way he was chewing his tie and being unkind to his hat I could tell he was agitated about something. This struck me as peculiar, because however hot Miles got inside he always presented a frozen exterior to the general public, like one of those comic *bombes* you get in French restaurants.

"Damn it, what are you doing like that?" he demanded suddenly. "Going round the place all day stark naked?"

"Just having the morning bath."

"Morning bath? But isn't it lunch time yet? I seem to have lost all sense of the clock."

He picked up the Empire State Building and made a few snowstorms, but it didn't seem to hold his attention much.

"An American chap gave me that in a pub," I explained quickly. "I wonder what on earth the white flaky stuff is they put inside to make the snow? Dandruff, do you suppose? Parmesan? I bet your young Bartholomew could tell us."

"Bartholomew?" growled Miles. "Bah."

This struck me as peculiar, too. Miles was generally bursting to pass on young Bartholomew's *obita dicta*, and generally give the impression it was only a matter of time before the lad had the painful choice between a seat in the Cabinet and opening for England at Lord's.

"I've just had Anemone on the phone," I went on brightly, trying to cheer up the conversation.

"Anemone? Bah."

"Here, I say," I returned. "That's no way for chaps to speak of the women chaps love."

Miles kicked his hat into the corner. "As far as I am concerned, all women can go to the devil."

I scratched my head. "But dash it! Only the other week you were carrying on again about the duties and delights of married life, and the basinful of bliss you were enjoying with Connie."

"I have left Connie," announced Miles.

"Left her?"

Miles snapped his fingers. "Like that."

"Good lord!"

This was even more startling. It was like Darby starting to phone Joan that he was persistently working late at the office.

"It is unnecessary to go into the distressing details." Miles had a bite at his tie. "I will content myself with merely mentioning that the whole matter is entirely Connie's fault."

"You don't mean she's been larking about with the milkman?"

"Milkman? Which milkman?"

"I mean, you could easily change your dairy—"

"I was sitting at my fireside, perfectly inoffensively reading *The Times*, which I am fond of doing after my day's work—I had been through a particularly trying operating list at St. Swithin's, I will add—when Connie suddenly rose from her chair and started to throw coconuts at me."

I felt a bit lost. "Coconuts?"

"Yes," said Miles. He went on to describe how she followed the coconuts up with *The Encyclopedia of Medical Sciences* (volume *Guts to Hydrophobia*), and while he dodged behind the piano made for the kitchen to find the eggs.

"Meanwhile, young Bartholomew, attracted by the noise, appeared downstairs with his teddy bear," Miles ended. "I fear the painful scene will leave a permanent scar on the child's personality. Though fortunately he seemed to be laughing heartily at the time. I then hid myself in the broom cupboard, and I have not spoken to Connie since."

"But my dear old Miles!" I gave a laugh. "You can't just up stakes because Connie chucked a few coconuts at you. Anyway, it's probably only some new parlor game she's seen on television."

Miles tightened his lips. "There's more to it than that. During the last few weeks Connie has been deliberately trying to kill young Bartholomew and me, not to mention herself. Now where do I sleep?"

I was by then feeling thoroughly confused, let alone half-frozen, but I could only point out there was hardly room in my flat to swing a kitten.

"I am of tidy habits and can manage perfectly well in a confined space," Miles countered. "You will remember at school I was always in charge of the camping."

He started to unpack.

"Look here, Miles, old lad, I already have to open the window for elbow room when cleaning my teeth—"

"Surely you don't expect me to sleep on the Embankment?"

"I just thought you might be rather more comfy on the Embankment, that's all."

"You still have my old camp bed, I believe? Then we can set it up and take turns to sleep on the divan. Week on, week off."

I didn't much like the sound of all those weeks. It was typical of my cousin Miles, expecting everyone to dash round and help whenever he got into a jam. It was just the same at school, every time he lost his football boots or got gummed up with his algebra. And I supposed that being a surgeon made it worse, because once you're scrubbed up in the theater, there're so many nurses scurrying about to tie up your gown and wipe your brow and order your coffee and biscuits, after a while you're apt to confuse asepsis with your own importance.

"But you'll never be able to run your practice from here, you chump," I pointed out. "There's all those phone calls from Harley Street, to start with."

"That is no problem. After last night, which I could fortunately spend in St. Swithin's on emergency duty, I started my summer holiday. Six weeks official National Health Service leave. Pity, I was rather looking forward to it."

There seemed no alternative to picking up some clothes and wedging myself in the kitchenette to dress. When I got back I found Miles had spread his belongings all over the divan and was rummaging among them anxiously.

"I've left my woolly slippers behind," he complained.

"It isn't far to go back and get them."

"I certainly shall not. Never in my life do I intend to speak to that woman Connie again."

I suddenly had one of those bright ideas of mine, which over the years have earned me a few quid at long odds just as they're coming under starter's orders. A few well-judged words from Uncle Grimsdyke, I felt, might settle their idiotic quarrel as quickly as my Empire State snowstorm. And that would not only restore Miles to a lifetime of bliss, but give me enough room for a bit of sleep as well.

"You make yourself at home," I invited warmly, "and I'll nip round to your house to collect the slippers. Or do you suppose Connie will start on me, too? Though if she's still got those eggs to throw, I haven't had my breakfast yet."

"Oh, very well," agreed Miles testily. "And while you're there you might as well bring along my dinner jacket, and my set of Dickens and my special shaving lotion as well."

Chapter Ten

After a night in an airplane it made a nice walk round to Miles's place. The English summer, with its genius for stage effects, had switched off the blasted heath scene and relit the set with soft golden watery sunshine, glistening prettily on the green leaves of the trees and the red sides of the buses and giving the pavements the look of freshly swabbed decks. I took a deep breath of damp London air. There's no place like home, I reflected, though it would be rather nicer if it had the New York licensing laws.

I crossed the Brompton Road feeling pretty worried. I wondered exactly what sort of monster had risen to the calm surface of Miles's marriage to rock the dream boat. Chucking coconuts about at home might be passed off as high spirits—after all, I bet Nell Gwynn and King Charles had no end of a time with those oranges—but from Miles's further remarks I wondered nervously if I'd find Connie answering the door with a blood-stained hatchet in her hand, reckoning how many strokes she would take to go round the entire family.

As it happened, she looked her usual calm and frilly self.

"Why, hello, Gaston." She smiled. "Quite a surprise visit."

"Yes, it is, rather."

"I expect you're looking for my dear husband?"

"Well—"

"I'm afraid he's out."

I nodded. "I know. He's just moved in with me."

"So that's where the little swine's bolted to, is it? Come inside."

I was relieved to find young Bartholomew in the hall, sucking an ice lolly as healthily as any kid in London. He'd hardly time to offer me a sporting lick before Connie bundled him away, and holding one hand to her forehead exclaimed, "The strain!"

"Yes, of course," I agreed for a start. "The strain."

"This last twenty-four hours. What I've suffered you'll never imagine."

"Now, don't worry, Connie," I said sympathizingly, patting her hand. "I'm perfectly certain I can get Miles back home again by dinnertime."

"Miles? I am now rid of Miles for good and all, thank you." She sounded as though the chap were a nasty attack of the shingles. "The strain is keeping it quiet from the neighbors. To think! How I consoled Sue next door, when her husband ran off with his secretary last Whitsun. Poor dear Sue! And now the little bitch is going to gloat like stink. Now that Miles has abandoned me and his child, penniless in a heartless world," she continued, going into the Regency drawing room and throwing herself on the Chippendale sofa. "Pour me out a large gin, Gaston, there's a dear."

Supposing this as good a treatment as any for a broken heart, I reached for the decanter.

After a couple of quick gulps Connie pointed out, "I have given Miles the best years of my life."

"Quite. But what was it exactly that—well, fired him into outer space?"

"You know what a nasty, narrow, sneaking suspicious character he's got?"

I did, but I supposed Connie knew even better, because Miles had lived with her for six years and he'd only just started with me.

"You must admit, he has some very fine qualities, old Miles," I murmured sportingly, trying offhand to think of one.

Connie swept her legs up on the sofa. "The man was simply trying to kill me. And Little Bartholomew. Not to mention himself."

I scratched my head again. I tried to picture the Miles ménage, with Connie upstairs polishing the top step and Miles downstairs sharpening up the bread knife on the back one. And what about young Bartholomew, I wondered, going about with the life expectancy of a prince in the Tower? I poured myself a gin too, subconsciously giving it a sniff for strychnine.

"It all started when Miles went for a week's fishing with Sir Lancelot," Connie announced, staring at the toes of her pretty little feet. "Sir Lancelot is apparently making an absolute fortune running some frightful racket in his house debloating capitalists."

I nodded.

"You know, Gaston, what a frightful hypochondriac Miles is?"

Noticing a half-empty box of chocolates beside her, Connie took up two or three.

"But a doctor who isn't a hypochondriac is as rare as a teetotal pub-keeper," I told her.

"I don't care in the slightest if Miles thinks he's got everything in the book from arthritis to Zambesi fever. I only object when he gives them to me. He came back from Sir Lancelot's all pink and rubbing his hands and saying we'd got to cut down on the calories. You can't see anything wrong with my figure, can you, Gaston?"

"Perfectly charming," I assured her.

"Oh, Miles carried on for days. He said obesity was the commonest nutritional disorder in the country, according to

the *British Medical Journal,* and that overfeeding children should
be punished as severely as starving them. Why, every time little
Bartholomew asked for some sweets he was told they rotted
his teeth and clogged his arteries. As for ice cream, Miles
wanted to put it on the schedule of poisons. Smoking, of course,
he'd forbidden months ago," Connie went on, lighting a cigarette. "Now he even stopped me having a little drink," she
ended, holding out her empty glass.

I began to see the point, which I felt was quite an advance on
Agatha Christie.

"He hasn't let me make a decent meal for weeks, and you
know how proud I am of my cooking. He even tried to organize morning exercises in Onslow Gardens, but thank heavens
the police objected. Then—" Connie hesitated—"one night
Miles went too far. He accused me of being unfaithful."

"Here, I say," I exclaimed, becoming rather more interested.

"With the apple pie," added Connie.

"With the—the what?"

"Oh, I was a fool, I suppose. When I thought he was asleep I
crept down to the fridge and finished off the apple pie. Miles
was absolutely furious. And then," she exclaimed triumphantly,
"do you know what? The very next day I caught the little
swine being immoral with the Camembert."

She helped herself to more chocs.

"Like all men, the toad came groveling and swearing he'd
never so much as look at another cheese again. And I," muttered
Connie into her second gin, "like a poor weak woman, forgave
him. Then a couple of nights ago he accused me of committing
misconduct with the sugar. I denied it. He said I had, he'd been
counting the lumps. Then the beast asked, what about my affair
with the coconut, at a hundred calories an ounce?

"Nutritious stuff, coconut."

"It so happens, Gaston, that at the moment I happen to be
rather fond of coconut. I lost my temper. I threw the coconuts

at him. Even then, the yellow-bellied little worm hid behind the
piano instead of taking it on the chest like a man. Oh, Gaston!"
exclaimed Connie, suddenly bursting into tears, "I'm so un-
happy. And so hungry."

"Tut," I said. "Tut, tut, tut."

What man can stand unmoved and watch a pretty girl
weeping over her chocolate creams? As she showed no signs
of drying up, I shifted on to the sofa and placed a brotherly arm
round her shoulders.

"Dear Gaston," sobbed Connie, "you're so sweet to me."

"Not at all. I'm only offering you the loan of my hanky."

"But Gaston, you *are* sweet." She laid a sisterly head on my
lapel. "You'll never know how I've tortured myself wondering whether . . . whether I really made the right choice."

"Bit late for going into that now, old girl," I murmured,
giving her right ear a fraternal stroke.

"Is it?" Connie sighed into my shirt front. "Is it?"

I swallowed. Miles may have known all about that apple pie,
but he didn't know how chummy I'd been with Connie before
he took her off to share his life in a hired Daimler. I'd seen her
first, when she was brought into St. Swithin's after a taxi
smash, still looking perfectly fetching with a Pott's fracture.
But as I was only a penniless student and Miles was already a
resident doctor, not only had he more glamour but he was
able to buy her better dinners as well. Also, Miles was a chap
with the hide and single-mindedness of a charging rhino, and
Connie was hardly out of plaster before accepting him.

I went about looking pretty cheesed off, like the knight who
was given such a rotten time of it by La Belle Dame Sans
Merci. No birds sang for a bit, certainly. But it's remarkably
easy to confuse the diagnosis of a broken heart with a scratch
from a playful kitten. Other girls came into my life, inspected
the premises, and decided on alternative accommodation elsewhere. By the time I was consoling her on the Chippendale

sofa, Connie was merely the lady who handed out the soup whenever Miles happened to ask me to dinner.

"I wonder so often," breathed Connie into my collar, "how life would have been had I married you instead, dear."

"A bit more cramped in my horses' larder."

"But so much more thrilling, Gaston! How romantic I remember you looked that lovely day you punted so beautifully up the river for a picnic."

Actually, it had been pouring with rain and I fell in twice, but Connie was getting her memories in Technicolor.

"And that gay weekend we had at Whortleton," Connie added.

Her Ma and Pa were there, and they only asked me along because they wanted someone to drive the car.

"You looked so lovely on the end of the pier," murmured Connie.

"Interesting spot, Whortleton."

Connie blew her nose. "And now my life is ruined and I shall never ever be happy again."

I patted her shoulder. "There, there. Come, come. Tut, tut."

"Oh, Gaston," breathed Connie, pushing aside the chocs and making herself more comfy. "You're such lovely ointment for a bruised soul."

At that moment I felt I'd better be going.

"Must you, Gaston? Come and see me again, dear." She stuck the handkerchief back in my pocket. "Otherwise I shall simply expire from loneliness. About six is the most convenient."

When I got into the street I realized I'd forgotten all about Miles's ruddy woolly slippers.

Chapter Eleven

"Gaston, how sweet of you to come."

It was a few hours later, and Lucy Squiffington was greeting me in a room that looked like a combined effort by the Antique Dealers' Fair and Chelsea Flower Show.

"And here," she added, indicating the chap in the baggy tweed suit on the sofa, seeing how many times he could twist his right leg around his left, "is George."

"Dear old Squiffy!" I cried.

He hadn't changed a bit. He was still a tall thin fellow with big glasses, hair like the stuffing in an Army mattress, and all his joints apparently held together with elastic bands. Squiffy had always gone about looking as though an arm or a leg were likely to drop off at any moment, and if it had he would never remember where he'd left it, being pretty absent-minded as well.

Naturally, we all three had a jolly good giggle about the dear old days at Whortleton. I couldn't stop that warm intragastric feeling coming back every time I took another look at Lucy, even though I kept reminding myself that I was present merely as the Squiffingtons' professional adviser. And I had to admit that poor old Squiffy himself was in something of a state. He'd always been a restless sort of bird, writhing about as though he'd just put on new woollen underwear. Now the poor fellow was as jumpy as a plate of snap-crackle-pop when you pour the milk on.

"Bashing atomic physics from nine to five must be no end of a strain," I suggested, feeling for a diagnosis over the teacups.

"It's all most frightfully secret, of course," said Squiffy, reaching for the cake. A greedy beggar he'd been at school, I remembered.

"Perhaps you'd explain the quantum theory to me when you have a moment? I'm afraid my own knowledge of physics pretty well ended on Archimedes' bath night."

"The quantum theory?" mumbled Squiffy through the cake. "I'm not at all certain that isn't on the secret list."

"But surely, George!" complained Lucy. "Must you always behave like an oyster with laryngitis? You could at least tell us where you're stationed."

"More than my life's worth. Top security. Yes, indeed! A lot of people would like to find out in—in—you-know-where."

"I suppose you must know the famous Sir James?" I hazarded.

"Oh, Jimmy? Yes, very well. Jolly good boss, too. Saw him only yesterday."

"Remarkable how quickly he's recovered from that bad car smash."

"Yes, it is, isn't it?"

"Considering it happened only last Saturday."

"Oh, yes?" said Squiffy.

"Out in Australia," I went on.

"You mean *that* Sir James?" asked Squiffy crossly. "Why didn't you say so in the first place?"

"I don't think we're being kind to George's nerves, Gaston."

"Let's stop talking shop," said Squiffy, trying to pout and eat cake at the same time.

Lucy patted my hand on the sofa. "Gaston will tell us ab-

solutely everything that happened since that awful nanny with
the moustache bundled me into the train at Whortleton."

I sat back to oblige, but I'd hardly opened my mouth before
a chap in a white jacket opened the door and announced, "Mr.
Basil Beauchamp."

"Basil Beauchamp!" I jumped up. "Oh no! You don't mean
the actor?"

"Of course," smiled Lucy. "Quite an honor, isn't it? Show
Mr. Beauchamp straight up."

I said nothing. For the second time this bounder Basil was
blighting my life. Another moment and he bounced in, all teeth
and carnation.

"What on earth are you doing here?" I asked at once.

"Good lord, Grim," returned Basil, the number of teeth on
view diminishing quickly. "But what on earth are *you* doing
here?"

"What, you two know each other?" asked Lucy, looking surprised.

"Know each other? Why Basil and I have been pals for
years and years. Haven't we, Basil? When I was a medical
student we used to share the same digs," I explained.

"*La Vie de Bohème,*" said Basil quickly. "Those carefree
prentice days." He gave a little laugh. "Yes, Dr. Grimsdyke
and I were indeed once *en garçon* in the same *atelier*. One leads
that sort of life while one is waiting for managements to discover one. I believe Dr. Grimsdyke still expresses his gratitude
for my tempering his own youthful excesses. It was I who kept
your nose to the midnight oil, eh, dear chappie? I say, what
gorgeous gladioli," said Basil, burying his nose in them and
changing the subject.

I felt my blood pressure leaving the launching pad. The chap
was nothing but a ruddy liar. Basil Beauchamp (pronounced
Beecham) might now be the famous actor, with a biscuit-
colored Rolls, his face on the sides of all the buses, and a rather

messy dish named after him in one of the posh West End restaurants. But in the days he rented the room next to mine his only audience was the landlady's daughter, who lashed him up with ham and cocoa in the kitchen when Mum was out, while he gave her Great Love Scenes from the Classics. And he'd have shifted to even tougher lodgings if I hadn't raised a few bob every quarter to repay those informal loans made to him by the local Gas Board, once he found how to fiddle the lock on his meter. That was why Basil never liked swapping jolly reminiscences when I bumped into him from time to time, particularly as I'd overheard everything the landlady had to say when she discovered where all that ham was going.

"But how wonderful that you should be old cronies." Lucy gave another smile. "Because Basil and I are very, very close friends indeed."

"Oh, are you?"

"Don't you think I'm a tremendously lucky girl, Gaston?"

"Lucky? Oh, yes. Of course."

Basil, who was still in the gladioli, seemed to think so too.

"That's still absolutely off the record you understand," he added quickly in my direction.

"Yet another of the afternoon's secrets." Lucy laughed.

"Those ghastly gossip columns," remarked Basil, shuddering.

"But Gaston would surely never breathe a word to the papers," declared Lucy.

"H'm," said Basil.

"You see, Basil's divorce isn't quite tied up yet. That's one of the reasons I went to New York. Dear Basil was kept here with his latest film, of course."

"Yes, I heard you'd been unloaded—been separated," I told him.

Before his starring days Basil had been taken on the household strength of some frightfully rich American woman in the capacity of husband, for which there happened to be a vacancy at the time, though I think he was relieved to find later it was only a temporary job, to go with her season in London.

"You must tell me all about those dreary lawyers in the car, my sweet," said Basil, seeming anxious to have Lucy elsewhere.

"Of course, darling. Basil's taking me to the dress rehearsal of a charity matinee we've been organizing for months and I'm absolutely thrilled." Lucy collected her bag and gloves. "There's nothing quite so exciting as the stage, is there?"

"Come along, my angel," urged Basil, giving me a bit of a glance. "Those poor players will be strutting and fretting, you know. Do remind me, dear chappie, to send you a couple of free seats, won't you?"

Another moment and they'd left me alone with Squiffy, still eating.

"Grim, old man," said Squiffy.

I made no reply. The interview had left me wallowing in a wave of nausea, particularly with the noise Squiffy was making over his cake.

"Grim, old man." Squiffy started to choke, indicating that he wanted to say something urgently. "I've some pretty dashed important news to tell you."

"Yes?" I wondered what it was Lucy put behind the ears to make her smell so nice.

"But it's a dead secret."

"Not another?"

"I mean, this is a real one." Squiffy scooped up the crumbs. "I've absolutely got to spill the beans to someone and I know I can confide in you, Grim. Do you remember how you kept quiet at school, when I slipped the Head's tea party that plate of hair-cream sandwiches? Besides, doctors have to keep secrets, don't they, or they get hauled up before the medical beaks? I'm afraid this is going to be a bit of a shock," he went on. "But— well, I'm not really an important scientist."

"No?"

"I'm a scientist, of course. Well, sort of . . . oh, dear!"

He got up and started striding about, arms and legs in all directions.

"It's all my old man's fault," he declared.

I helped myself to another cup of tea.

"You know what he's like, Grim?"

"A bit of a tough egg, he struck me."

I hadn't seen Pa Squiffington since I buried him in the sand at Whortleton. Though I'd often thought of the old boy while looking for the racing news in the paper and spotting the item headed "City Notes," which generally says something like, "There was much calling for money in Lombard Street today." There goes poor old Pa Squiffington, I told myself, up and down the gutter hollering at the open windows, buttonholing chaps in tophats, trying to touch the copper directing the traffic, ending up on the doorstep with his bowler hung out hopefully.

I gathered Squiffington's Bank wasn't one of the common sort with a counter downstairs, where they take the cash from all comers. According to Squiffy, who'd often prowled the corridors optimistically, they never handled the vulgar stuff at all. Financial wizards—if it was a nice morning and they'd holed all their putts on Saturday—simply told their secretaries to send it round a million. And if Pa Squiffington never saw it being unpacked, Squiffy certainly didn't see it at all. His father was one of those lean athletic executives, whose idea of a rip-roaring evening, I remembered from Whortleton, was a game of chess and a chocolate biscuit with his Ovaltine.

"You know the old man wanted me to be a doctor," Squiffy went on, absently cutting another piece of cake. "The great-grandad who founded the bank—that's the one over the fire-place with the face like the underdone steak with side whiskers —was the son of a doctor in Canada, who got no end of a name stalking about in blizzards patching up people eaten by bears. I was obviously a frightful duffer at business—you remember at school I could never work out what those tedious chaps A, B, and C owed each other after those rather shifty deals in compound interest. But for some reason the medical schools didn't agree with the old man, so he packed me off to Canada for a year or two. When I came back he announced that I should be a scientist, science being all the thing."

"They're even teaching it these days at Eton."

"I think Dad already saw me stepping up for the Nobel Prize," Squiffy went on. "But of course one has to make a start somewhere, and after going round a few universities I was finally enrolled up at Mireborough—oddly enough, just after the old man had donated a new boathouse. They were pretty tough toward me at Mireborough, with their northern independence and all that," he added morosely. "Even after the old man had donated a new library—he rather fancies himself as a pocket Rockefeller, you know. And as he'd recently donated a new chemistry laboratory I really can't see why they made such a fuss just because I burnt the old one down."

Squiffy sprawled in his chair.

"It was in the practical exam, and I don't know what went wrong, quite. They shouldn't set such damn fool questions, I suppose. The Fire Brigade had hardly cleared up before they told me it would be cheaper for the university all round if I left. Luckily, the old man had just set off for Karachi, but I had to find a job—he never donates anything to me, of course. A bit tricky it was, too, as I wasn't even a B.Sc(Mire.). Luckily, a fellow in my year tipped me for one in the middle of Dorset."

"Not meddling with the government's atoms?" I asked nervously, feeling that next time Squiffy blew anything up he'd do it properly.

"Actually, I'm a stinks beak in a prep school," he confessed. "The ruddy chemistry master. A miserable hole it is, too. The Head's got the outlook of an undertaker with an overdraft—

charges for test tubes and chemicals, and probably for use of force of gravity as well. But that's only half the trouble."

He paused, and having finished all the cake started on his nails.

"You see, Grim—good lord, is that the time?" Squiffy jumped up. "I'll miss my train, and there'll be the most almighty row if I'm late. What do you think of that fellow Beauchamp?" he added, bolting for the door. "In my opinion he's a bit of a stinker."

"Yes, he's a bit of a stinker in my opinion, too."

"Not at all the sort of fellow I'd like to see Lucy fixed up with," Squiffy continued, disappearing.

"Not at all the sort of fellow I'd like to see her fixed up with, either," I agreed.

Though why, I asked, finding myself alone among the remains of the tea and the gladioli, should I worry what fellow Lucy got herself fixed up with? I didn't care a rap if she was a very, very close friend of every male performer in Shaftesbury Avenue and Bertram Mills Circus. I was, I told myself, no more concerned with the affair than if I were watching Basil canoodling with his leading lady beyond the footlights. I swallowed the last of my tea and left. After all, I was perfectly happily engaged, to quite the nicest girl in the world.

Chapter Twelve

"I'm afraid I didn't bring your woolly slippers," I apologized to Miles back in my Chelsea flat. "Connie didn't seem able to lay hands on them."

My cousin was out when I'd returned earlier from calling on his distraught missus, a note under the milk merely saying, "Unexpectedly summoned to St. Swithin's. Shall be back this evening. I like to dine about seven, and please remember I am allergic to chicken and kidneys."

"Woolly slippers? I don't think I shall be wanting my woolly slippers after all," said Miles.

I edged beside him on the divan. I felt I hadn't been much help to Squiffy over tea, and now I wondered how to bring the pair of ruffled lovebirds together over supper. Connie was one of the best, I reflected. A charming and devoted girl, though perhaps with latent tendencies to nestle up to young men. And even old Miles wasn't a bad chap at heart, despite his distressing habit of regarding me as something found under the table after one of those Babylonian orgies.

"Now look here, Miles, old lad—" I started.

I'd already decided only half his domestic trouble came from the idiot going about like a dietetic Hitler. All married couples get browned off with each other from time to time, with no ill effects beyond a few slammed doors and a kick or two at the dog, but when they've got a starvation-level blood sugar as well they're likely to suffer more acute symptoms.

"Miles, old man, talking as chap to chap—" I tried again.

I paused. The difficulty was finding the right treatment. Marital disharmonies turn up twice a day in general practice, disguised as anything from mania to myopia. But our British medical schools, though jolly hot on such solid stuff as fractures and ruptures, don't leave you better trained for handling them except by advising the husband to take up golf and the wife to interest herself in local politics.

"The dinner jacket might have been useful, though," was all Miles said, coughing a bit.

I was surprised to notice him smoking one of my cigarettes.

"That's the first time I've seen you with a fag in your mouth since the night you celebrated your Mastership at Oxford by letting down the Junior Dean's bicycle tires," I told him.

"And it won't be the last," returned Miles calmly. He gave me a leer, brought short by his coughing a bit more. "How about an—ah—quick snort?"

I stared at him. "But you never drink except at Christmas."

"I do now. I definitely feel like an—er—swift noggin. Eh?"

I shrugged my shoulders. Remembering that I was the chap's host whatever, I produced the remains of the Scotch from under the kitchen sink.

"Here's cheers, down the hatch, bottoms up, lovely grub, and the best of British luck," said Miles.

"Look here," I asked, when he'd finished spluttering. "Are you feeling quite all right? I mean, the mental strain of the past few days—"

"I feel," explained Miles briefly, "like a man reborn. I have passed the day examining my soul," he informed me. "For years I have lived a life of austerity and respectability as a model husband. What boots it to a heartless female like Connie? She has forced me to leave her and become a grass widower. So

I intend to damn well behave like a grass widower. How about another—ah—doch and doris for the road?"

"I should take it easy," I advised, pouring him a small one. "For a chap who's just been reborn you've got past the weaning stage pretty smartly."

"Tonight—" Miles gave a wink. "Tonight we shall go out and—um—pick up some crumpet. Yes, definitely! We shall hit the town and grab ourselves a bit of snicket. What the devil are you laughing about?" he demanded crossly.

"Sorry, old lad," I apologized. "It's just that you strike me like Mrs. Grundy doing a striptease."

"Striptease, that's the ticket!" exclaimed Miles at once. "I've always wanted to see some. I never got a chance when I was on the Morality Commission. The Bishop always pinched the striptease."

"My dear old Miles," I protested, not much caring to share the tiles that night with my cousin. "Don't you think you could postpone your descent to the underworld until tomorrow? I've just got in from a very exhausting journey."

"Cheltenham isn't far."

"No, I suppose it isn't," I admitted. "Anyway, if you hit the night spots someone's bound to recognize you. These places are always full of the very last people you expect to meet. And if it ever got back to St. Swithin's—"

"I've thought of that." Miles drew a large pair of dark glasses from his pocket. "With these I shall be totally unrecognizable. See? I believe it is how all the film stars disguise themselves when attending their haunts of vice."

Actually, he just looked like Miles in sunglasses, but I said, "Oh, all right. If you really want to paint the town red, I suppose I'd better come along to see you keep your brush clean."

"By the way," ended Miles, stubbing out his cigarette, "where does one find a bookie? I have an overwhelming desire to place a flutter on a horse."

I suppose I should have realized from the start that Miles's inhibitions were snapping like old elastic bands. Particularly once he put on his dark glasses, and for some reason he imagined that because he could hardly see anything through them nobody could see him at all.

"Take me to a pub," he demanded. "I have always wanted to go to a pub."

"Anything to oblige, old lad."

I felt we could do no better than my local, one of those clean and cozy little pubs you're sometimes lucky enough to come across in London, which give the impression of the landlord providing drinks for passers-by in his front parlor. It was patronized by such solid citizens as policemen, postmen, and commissionaires, and run by a very decent middle-aged couple, an ex-Guardsman and his wife with arthritis, who always extended me a warm welcome and sometimes credit as well.

"Good evening, Mrs. Hildenborough," I greeted the landlady across the bar.

"Good evening, Doctor. Quite a stranger."

"I've been visiting relatives in Cheltenham. Two pints, please."

Miles leaned over the counter. "Good evening, duckie," he said, almost catching her jumper with his glasses.

Mrs. Hildenborough looked rather surprised, but returned politely, "Good evening. Is that all right for your blind friend?" she added, putting the pint carefully near Miles's elbow.

"I call the meeting to order," announced Miles.

"You what, old lad?"

"I'll pay. Isn't that what you say?"

"You mean you're in the chair."

"That's it. Dear me," he announced, feeling in his pocket. "My wallet. It's in my other jacket, up in your flat."

"I'll get it," I told him, having no intention of paying the fare as well as conducting the tour. "It won't take a minute. Don't drink my pint as well."

I soon found Miles's wallet, but I ran into the old dear who cleans the stairs leading from the converted horses' dining room, who wanted her usual chat about her kidneys. By the time I'd dispensed professional advice I was rather worried that my cousin might be feeling embarrassed in his strange surroundings.

As it happened, I reached the pub just as he sailed through the door on to the pavement, followed by Mr. Hildenborough wiping his hands.

"I don't want to see you inside my house again, you nasty piece of work," shouted the landlord. "And that goes for you too, Dr. Grimsdyke. If that's the sort of company you mix with, I don't want any of it under my roof, thank you."

"Here, I say." I stared blankly as Miles picked himself up. "But what on earth happened, Mr. Hildenborough? Did he spit in someone's beer, or something?"

"He insulted Mrs. Hildenborough," announced the landlord. "That's what. He's lucky I didn't bash his face in. Now clear off the pair of you, before I call the police."

"But we haven't paid for our beer—" I exclaimed.

"Keep your immoral earnings to yourself," snapped Mr. Hildenborough, slamming the pub door.

"What the devil have you been up to, Miles?" I demanded.

"This is real low life, isn't it?" He dusted his trousers, not seeming at all disconcerted. "That man is what you call a 'bouncer,' I believe? A pity I was bounced just as I was starting to enjoy myself. Naturally, I wasn't serious in my proposition to the barmaid. I suppose I didn't offer her enough."

"You didn't offer—? Good lord, old lad! You don't mean you suggested to Mrs. Hildenborough—?"

"That sort of thing is always on the cards with barmaids, isn't it? I gave her a little pinch as she turned to pour some spirits, and the bouncer appeared. Where shall we go now?

How about the striptease? I particularly want to visit that theater near Piccadilly, called the Waterwheel."

Feeling I'd better get Miles out of the district as soon as possible, I pushed him into a taxi and instead of the Waterwheel took him to one of those nonstop shows in Soho, where they have a simple little program of a chap coming on and doing conjuring tricks, then a skinny girl appearing and taking her clothes off, then another chap doing conjuring tricks, followed by another skinny girl, and so on. But Miles seemed rather disappointed, I suppose because he saw much the same thing every week in women's outpatients, though personally I thought the conjuring tricks were rather crafty.

"And now," Miles announced in Old Compton Street, after the first skinny girl had turned up again, "you must take me to see the Real Thing."

"Real thing? What real thing?"

"The real low life." He gave another of his leers and dug me in the ribs. "*You* know."

I gave a sigh. Like tourists anywhere from Reykjavik to Rio de Janeiro, Miles believed there was some terrific low show somewhere patronized only by the natives, enough to keep anyone in memories for years and years of winter evenings. Actually, the natives are always at home watching the telly and filling up their football pools, but Miles went on insisting I take him to the Real Place in the West End.

"It is an establishment I never had the chance to see for the Royal Commission," he explained. "I'm afraid the others rather fobbed me off with the jails."

After a few drinks and a bag of potato chips in another pub, the simplest solution struck me was taking the idiot to a perfectly respectable night club I knew near Berkeley Square. As this was an expensive joint, and the amount of candle power provided in such places always varies inversely with the prices, it would be too dark for Miles to make much of it anyway. And that wasn't to mention the dark glasses.

In the night club, the head waiter led us through the crowd on the dance floor to a table next to the band, Miles ordering the champagne before we'd got through the doorway. After a couple of glasses he perked up again, and started asking for the crumpet.

"There isn't any," I told him, becoming rather short. "You have to bring your own. The management only provides the booze and atmosphere."

"But there's a lovely little piece of stuff over there." Miles pointed across the dance floor. "That little brunette, sitting all alone."

I turned to look, but at that moment the band exploded and everybody jumped up to dance.

"Just my type," said Miles, rubbing his hands. "Not only charming, I would say, but intelligent. How do I set about it?"

"Set about what?"

"Why, dating her down, of course."

"Dating her up."

"That's it. What happens to be the customary procedure?"

"You can slip the waiter a quid and ask him to take a message," I told him, now thoroughly fed up with the outing, not to mention half-asleep on my feet. "But I shouldn't bother, because she's bound to be here with some Guards' officer, or lord, or something, who will only come over and do you."

Before I could stop him, Miles grabbed a passing waiter by the coattails and pressed a quid into his hand with the instructions, "Kindly inform the dark lady in glasses at the table exactly opposite that I have fallen violently in love with her."

"Very good, sir."

"Now you've done it," I said in alarm, glancing quickly toward the fire escape behind us. "She'll probably send for the management, and that'll make the second time you've been chucked out tonight."

"I am surprised at you, Gaston," returned Miles airily. "Quite surprised. You have no initiative, no daring. I distinctly saw the girl smile at me in a most inviting manner. Just you wait and see."

"Look here, Miles, this is Berkeley Square, not Buenos Aires—"

The waiter reappeared. "The lady says thank you, sir, and that you are her dream boy, sir."

"What did I tell you?" beamed Miles. He slipped the waiter another quid. "Ask the lady if she will make me deliriously happy forever by joining our table."

"Very good, sir."

"I really believe, Gaston," said Miles smugly, "that you'd no idea I had such attraction for the ladies. Believe me, that is far from the case."

"That was a pretty smooth pickup, I must say," I admitted.

"I have, I consider, quite a reasonable ration of what they call sex appeal. I am not particularly bad looking, and I have charming manners and plenty of not only entertaining but intelligent conversation. Were it not for my rather attractive shyness, I could make no end of conquests with the fair sex."

"You can start now," I told him. "Here she comes."

"My dear," Miles rose to his feet, bowing so low he pretty well knocked the ice bucket for six. "How perfectly charming."

"But I'm enchanted," said the girl in the dark glasses, offering her hand.

Then they had a better look at each other.

"Connie!" exploded Miles. "What the devil are you doing in this—this sink of iniquity?"

"Miles, you little toad! And what, may I ask, are you doing in it, too?"

"Gaston dragged me here," said Miles quickly. "And there

you are, letting yourself be accosted by strange men with the lowest intentions—"

Connie stamped her foot. "You beast! So those were your intentions toward a defenseless female all alone, were they?"

"I don't mean that at all," snapped Miles. "You were sitting there deliberately seducing me. Your own husband, too! It's about the limit."

"Go to hell," said Connie, clocking him with the champagne bottle.

There was a bit of a scene after that, but I didn't care. I'd already opted out of it through the fire escape. The time had come, I felt, for Grimsdyke's crowded day to draw to its close.

Chapter Thirteen

"My life," announced Miles, while shaving the next morning, "will never be the same again."

"Well, your face is going to be rather different for a bit, to start with," I told him.

Miles squinted into the mirror at his features, which were undergoing alterations.

"It is indeed unfortunate I have incurred a periorbital hematoma of such proportions," he admitted. "Though should anyone question me on the causation of the injury, I am glad to say I have already invented a highly ingenious excuse."

"I was thinking of a bit of steak for dinner," I intimated. "If you like, you can take yours externally instead."

I'd hardly heard my cousin let himself in and fall over the camp bed. Those flights across the Atlantic at a hundred miles a martini are all very well, but they leave you pretty exhausted afterwards, particularly when you have to reset yourself from New York time to the British summer sort. I suppose I should have been a decent chap and stayed in the night club to pacify the sinister-looking birds in dinner jackets who always advance purposefully from the shadows on such occasions. Or I might have waited up with my checkbook in case he wanted bailing out, particularly as I'd already established the drill for such occasions. But my only feeling on reaching home was the pretty base one of being damn lucky to have first go at the divan.

"I must say, I don't quite grasp the clinical history of your injuries," I told Miles, starting to boil a couple of eggs. "That ruddy great bump on your occiput I know was Connie with the champagne. Did she follow up with the mixed bag of contusions and cuts on the mandibular region?"

"The minor traumata," said Miles calmly, lathering between them, "were inflicted by the person who has deposed myself from the throne of Connie's affections."

"Oh, yes?" I upended the egg timer.

My cousin described at length how some dark, smooth chap, returning from the telephone to find his partner flailing the air with champagne bottles, crossed the dance floor and knocked Miles among the hors d'oeuvres with no questions asked.

"Fortunately, I recovered myself." He gave a chilly smile through the soap. "I was able to disable Connie's gigolo with a blow in the epigastric region."

"But Miles, you chump! How do you know it wasn't one of Connie's relatives, or some old friend of the family?"

"I know Connie's relatives very well. They all stay with us frequently for considerable periods. And Connie would never make friends I did not approve of." Miles gave a little laugh. "Now she is free to make acquaintances as undesirable as she may wish, as I have resolved that a divorce is inevitable."

"Look here," I insisted, loading the toaster, "even with a shocking hangover you can't seriously think of divorcing Connie?"

"I had decided on it even before the management of that place escorted me in such an undignified manner to the garbage lift. I fancy I have fishbones and potato skins attached to my waistcoat still."

"Think what an idiot you'll look standing up in court, when the judge says, 'What grounds?' and you say, 'She socked me on the noggin with my bottle of Bollinger, m'lud.' A fat lot of sympathy you'll get for that."

"You overlook the Other Man."

"Dash it! I bet that was absolutely aboveboard, knowing Connie as I do. I mean, knowing all you've told me about Connie."

"I like my eggs lightly boiled," said Miles sitting down.

My cousin was a silent eater, who demolished his breakfast as steadily as he got through everything that confronted him during the rest of the day. It was only when he'd wiped the remains of the marmalade from his little bristly moustache he announced:

"That was three hundred and fifty calories. If you imagine, Gaston, that I shall petition for a divorce from Connie on the grounds of cruelty, you are mistaken."

"I suppose you can get one for desertion, but some lawyer chap once told me you have to keep it up for three solid years," I returned, quickly working out that meant eighteen months for me on the camp bed.

"I propose to obtain a divorce on the grounds of my marital infidelity."

I looked at my cousin—sitting across my draughtboard-sized table bashing his empty eggshell with a spoon—in a new light.

"Miles, you old dog! All these years you've been keeping to yourself some piece of private poppet—"

"How dare you, Gaston! It is simply that—in spite of Connie's outrageous behavior—I intend to act like a gentleman. I gather from the newspapers one can arrange such things."

"Look here, old lad—don't you think you should have a word with your solicitor?"

"I should prefer to keep out of the hands of my solicitor. Also, he happens to be Connie's brother. No, my dear Gaston. I intend to leave the organization of the whole matter to you."

"To me? But dash it, what the devil do I know about divorces?"

"A great deal, I should imagine, as you move freely in the

demimonde where such events are not only commonplace but customary. The entire affair must be completed before the end of my holiday, as I should be far too busy at St. Swithin's to attend to it. And you will observe the greatest discretion. Doctors do not make popular divorcees, and vice versa. In particular, it must not reach the ears of Mr. Zeus Odysseus—you know, the wealthy Greek gentleman."

I nodded. "Everyone who can read the papers knows Mr. Odysseus."

"Dame Hilda was privileged to meet him while attending the International Delinquency Congress in Athens, and left him agreeably disposed toward donating a considerable sum for an institution here to study juvenile delinquency. Of which I, naturally, should be the director. Mr. Odysseus is shortly arriving here to approve the plans. It is a scheme dear to Dame Hilda's heart, and—strictly between ourselves—even the heart of the Prime Minister." Miles finished his coffee. "You may see me a life peer yet, Gaston, eh? Ha, ha!"

"Ha, ha," I said.

"I should not like Mr. Odysseus to think my private life nurtured any scandal."

"I shouldn't think a divorce one way or another would worry the chap much," I told him. "I forget whether over the years he's accumulated more missuses or millions."

"I must now step down to Lloyds, as I have already heard a rumor that his yacht had been sighted approaching the cliffs of Dover. You might let me know this evening, Gaston, exactly what I am obliged to do in order to act like a gentleman. Where is my spare pair of dark glasses?"

Miles froze. A terrific knocking sounded on the front door.

"Not someone from the night club . . . ?"

"Oh, it's probably only the postman with the usual armful of free samples from the drug firms."

On the mat was Sir Lancelot.

"Good morning, Grimsdyke. I hope I— Good God, what's he doing here?" he asked, staring at Miles.

Miles gave a weak grin. "I had dropped in to discuss some professional matters with Gaston."

"Not this hour of the day?"

I rallied round. "Over a working breakfast, sir."

"H'm. Who gave you that ruddy great black eye?"

"As a matter of fact," said Miles, quickly donning his glasses, "I happened to be going upstairs in the dark and ran into a door."

"Yes," said Sir Lancelot, "and the housemaid's baby came from a gooseberry bush. Who caught him one, Grimsdyke? A dissatisfied patient or a dissatisfied husband?"

Miles gave another grin, picked up his hat, and murmuring something about an urgent case bolted downstairs.

"I am totally at a loss to understand what is going on," declared Sir Lancelot. "However, it is no concern of mine. As I was spending the night at my Harley Street flat I called to discover how the New York conference ended."

"I've got most of the report here, sir. Didn't have time to finish it yesterday, I'm afraid. Rather a full day."

"My dear feller, there is no urgency. I fear I have shut down my clinic. My wife," he explained, stroking his beard, "raised certain objections, I cannot understand why. However, as I must maintain some form of activity to keep my house and my fishing rights, I intend to reopen it as a center for maladjusted teen-agers."

"Teen-agers, sir?"

"Yes. They're all the rage these days. When I was young, of course, teen-agers hadn't been invented and juveniles were regarded as being maladjusted as a matter of course. In my view, all adolescents should be given a thoroughly beastly time of it, in order to leave them something to look forward to when they grow up."

"Quite, sir. Cup of coffee, sir?"

"I have breakfasted, thank you. I'm afraid my views have already caused me to cross swords with Dame Hilda Parkhouse, one of my wife's rather ghastly friends—"

"Yes, sir. I'm engaged to her daughter, sir."

"And so you are. So you are."

"What's the joke, sir?" I asked, observing him grinning broadly.

"I'm afraid you wouldn't see it, Grimsdyke. No, you obviously wouldn't see it. You noticed my letter on juvenile delinquency in *The Times* this morning?"

"I'm afraid Miles hogged *The Times*. He left his at home, sir," I added quickly.

"You sleep in two beds, I see, Grimsdyke?"

"Yes, sir. I get rather restless. I like to slip into a nice cool one halfway through the night."

"H'm."

"And—er, by the way, sir, perhaps you wouldn't mention to Dame Hilda that I was with you in New York?"

"H'm."

"I wanted to break it to her myself as a surprise, sir."

Sir Lancelot gave a sigh. "I must be looking old. Nobody even bothers to deceive me properly any more. Very well, Grimsdyke. Post the report to Wales. And I'd recommend cold compresses for that eye."

Sir Lancelot left. I shoveled up the remains of the eggs, feeling that Miles was an idiot. Not that it would disqualify him from the House of Lords, I supposed, judging by some of the speeches they make there from time to time. Miles had no more intention of divorcing Connie, I told myself as I licked the marmalade spoon, than of resigning from the staff of St. Swithin's. And being such a self-centered bird he regarded both as much the same procedure.

Poor old Miles! I tossed out the toast crumbs for the birds.

Such an intellectual force with his surgery and sociology, now just as infantile as any other narked husband. Driving cars and matrimony, I reflected—there's nothing like either for reducing us all to the same common denominator.

But I hadn't time to ponder more about my cousin's domestic problems because I had to be off to work.

Chapter Fourteen

It was good to hear the doorman greet me as I arrived, "Nice morning, Dr. Grimsdyke. Glad to see you with us again."

"Good morning, Harry," I returned affably. "Everything pottering along all right without me?"

"I think they managed somehow, Doctor. But I've an urgent message waiting."

"Oh, yes?"

"Will you go straight upstairs, sir? They don't want to start the big heart operation unless you're there."

"H'm. Do they actually want me to perform it?"

"I fancy they only want you on the spot to give advice, sir."

"Very well, Harry. Anything good for today's card at Kempton Park?"

"I wouldn't like to trust myself today, Doctor."

I must say it felt fine to be back, particularly as summer was right on the job again and providing a sparkling sunny June morning, with the mercury already shooting up like the hollyhocks. I marched briskly down the long main corridor, swapping hellos with the porters and the chaps who pushed the trolleys and the pretty little secretaries and the girls who brought round the tea. I was even whistling a bit as I reached the staff lift and ran into the Chief's secretary herself.

"Why, hello, Dr. Grimsdyke. Good trip to New York?"

"Very instructive, thank you."

"I think the Chief would like you to drop in before leaving, Doctor."

I frowned. "Nothing wrong, I hope?"

"Oh, no, Dr. Grimsdyke. Quite the reverse. He was absolutely delighted with the big brain operation you did before going away."

"Glad I came up to scratch. Great inspiration the Chief, of course," I added, lobbing the compliment back.

The secretary turned over her notebook. "You've got the big grafting operation next week, Dr. Grimsdyke. Will you require the artificial kidney?"

I nodded. "Definitely the artificial kidney."

"I'll arrange for it. The Chief wants to know if he can leave working it to you?"

"Entirely," I told her.

She smiled. "He'll be delighted to hear that, Doctor."

I smiled back, pressed the button, and went up.

Pushing open the door at the top, I found myself in the familiar operating theater with the big shadowless lamp, the shiny table, the same little nurses scurrying among the dressing bins, and the same registrar and houseman, already scrubbed up and waiting.

"Hello, Dr. Grimsdyke," said everyone. "Good to see you back."

"What ho, all," I returned.

"I'm just about to start one of those hole-in-the-heart operations," announced the surgeon through his mask. "I wonder if you'd mind giving me a bit of advice?"

"Yes, certainly, old lad. What do you want to know?"

"Well—what sort of incision do I make, for a start?"

"Oh, from here to here," I explained, crossing to the patient. "Just make a ruddy great slit."

"A ruddy great slit will do, eh?"

"Yes, and the houseman will be ready with clips and so on, to stop the hemorrhage."

"Thanks." The surgeon nodded. "Darling," he asked the theater sister, "have you got all the right instruments?"

"There's not much point in starting now," objected the registrar. "It's almost time for the tea to come up."

"I could certainly do with a nice cup of char," agreed the surgeon.

"So could I," said the patient, getting off the operating table.

"There's a break for a commercial here, anyway," added the theater sister.

"Rehearse again in fifteen minutes," called the producer through the intercom. "Thanks for putting us right, Dr. Grimsdyke."

I must say, it was a job that kept you on your toes. One mistake in the operating theater and you heard about it for weeks. Gone are the times when a chap could remove an appendix with half a pair of obstetrical forceps and the thing you use for looking at eardrums. The surgeon today has only to choose the wrong strength of catgut and people start writing indignant letters before you can say Whatnot Washes Whiter. Hence my job as technical adviser to "Ambulance Entrance," which as everyone knows pretty well brings the entire nation to a standstill from seven to half-past on Wednesday evenings. Though how anyone can relax after a heavy day by putting up his feet in the parlor and watching people pulling out socking great tumors among torrents of blood is totally beyond me.

"I'll show them how to give the anesthetic and put on the bandages after the tea break," I explained to the producer. "I must just nip down to see someone in the dressing rooms."

I made my way across the television-studio floor, cluttered with those book-lined studies where chaps hold forth about the political situation, and which are really only bits of painted cardboard. Then I cut through the studio next door where they were rehearsing the big spectacular show, which pretty well brings the entire nation to a standstill from eight-thirty to nine on Saturdays.

"Why, there's the doctor," said a voice, as I picked my way among the girls in ostrich feathers drinking tea. "Hello, Doctor! How goes it?"

"Why, hello, Gertrude," I returned. "How's the old back?"

"Not so dusty, thank you, duckie. I do get a twinge from time to time, of course. Anno domini, I suppose. None of us are getting any younger, are we? Though we all try to pretend we are in this business. Did you hear the bad news?"

"Bad news? I'm afraid I've been away."

"They're dropping our act from the show."

"Oh, no!" I sympathized. "Why, it's like dropping the three witches from *Macbeth*. I mean, parts of the same importance—"

"Joan and Cissy are out phoning our agent this very moment. I expect something will turn up."

"Yes, I'm sure it will," I consoled her, "with a brilliant act like yours. You wait till people write in, the very first Saturday you're not among those present in the sitting room."

"If it hadn't been for you, Doctor, we shouldn't have been in the show as long as this. And that's a fact."

"Oh, come," I said. "Come, come."

The great thing about my job on television—apart from having to work only once a week—was all the rather jolly actors and actresses I met. Gertie Piggott was one of the Three Jellybone Sisters, who did contortions, and I'd been called urgently from supervising a big amputation operation next door when she got stuck one night with the back of her head touching her heels. I'd earned the undying gratitude of all three by unsticking her, particularly as it was the end of the performance and they'd have had no end of trouble getting her home in the bus.

I couldn't sympathize more with the poor dear about getting

the sack, because I noticed Evan Crippen making his way towards me among the Television Tappers.

Everyone, of course, knows Evan Crippen. Occasionally he comes across someone who doesn't, and he takes on a look of mixed horror and pity, like some broad-minded missionary coming across the chaps eating their grandmother. Evan Crippen is one of our top telly interviewers, as much a product of the age as deep-frozen fish and the hydrogen bomb. Those famous programs of his, you may remember, used to end up with admirals shaking at the knees, famous actors in tears, judges white in the face, and Cabinet ministers carried out on stretchers.

"Hello, there, Doctor," Evan drawled. A smile crossed his thin features, with their well-known expression of a conscientious sanitary inspector on holiday in southern Europe. "Did you see my program last week?"

"I was away in New York, I'm afraid."

"Oh, rotten luck. I believe you know this fellow Sir Lancelot Spratt?" he asked, coming straight to business.

I nodded.

"I see from the papers he's climbing on the delinquency band wagon. If I could get him and Dame Hilda Parkhouse together on "This Evening," it might make quite an interview, don't you think?"

I felt myself it would be like a couple of mastodons jumping the lights at the crossroads, but I only nodded again.

"Dame Hilda's keen, if you can persuade the old boy."

"I'll have a try, if you like," I promised halfheartedly.

"Thanks, Doctor. Must rush off, I'm afraid. Got to look up some dirt on a field marshal."

I rushed off, too. I didn't much care for exposing Sir Lancelot to Evan Crippen and those quiet questions of his, like a good dentist going steadily through a mouthful of teeth. But, I reflected, Dame Hilda was my impending mother-in-law, and better men than Sir Lancelot were nightly airing their views and baring their souls across everybody's hearth rug. I couldn't ponder on this more deeply at the time, because I'd reached the door with MR. BASIL BEAUCHAMP on it.

A girl's scream rang through the woodwork, followed by a gasp of, "Kill me tomorrow! Let me live tonight."

I didn't know quite what to do, but I thought I'd better knock.

"Come in," said Basil.

The actor was reclining on a couch in a pink silk dressing gown, surrounded by vases of roses and smoking a cigar. In an armchair beside all the sticks of grease paint and telegrams from his admirers sat Lucy Squiffington.

"Why, Gaston, darling!" exclaimed Lucy. "We meet again."

"Ah, dear chappie," said Basil, eyeing me like an unfavorable notice in the Sunday papers.

"Perhaps I intrude?"

"Not a bit." Lucy smiled. "Basil was taking me through the death scene in *Othello*. Isn't it wonderful, he's teaching me to act? We'd half-finished *Anthony and Cleopatra* in the drawing room before I went off to New York."

"Lucy has become utterly passionate about the theater. Ever since we first met at the Actors' Orphanage Ball."

"And once Daddy gets home, I'm sure I can persuade him to finance Basil's wonderful new production of *Saint Joan*."

"As a musical," added Basil.

As far as I remembered, Lucy could never persuade him to finance even a second ice cream, but I said nothing.

"I'm so thrilled, Gaston. Basil says if I stick to my lessons I might even get the big part."

"I want someone absolutely sweet and saintlike," mentioned Basil. "And it's remarkable how few of our leading ladies are. Just the occasion, I feel, for someone absolutely unknown."

"Basil, I—"

"Let me tell you my ideas for the production, dear chappie."
Like all actors, Basil rather ignored the cues once talking about
himself. "I intend to start with myself on the stage—all by
myself—and I shall then deliver a speech, to myself—"

"Basil," I interrupted firmly. "I'm only here for a little advice. But if you like I'll come back after class."

"Advice?" Basil looked as though I had let down the curtain
on him. "Some production problem in that grisly little show
of yours?"

"No." I glanced at Lucy. "It's rather on the delicate side.
Though, as a matter of fact," I added, remembering New
York, "Lucy might be able to help. It's about a divorce."

"Gaston! On the plane you never told me you were married."

"It's for a friend."

Basil blew a jet of cigar smoke. "Never, never, dear chappie,
let yourself become involved in the matrimonial affairs of
others. It's much less dangerous to stop a decent cosh fight
any day."

"I rather promised. And as you've recently had a bit of rehearsing in that sort of show—"

"I think my dear wife just goes down to Las Vegas, where
you get them from a slot machine," he said doubtfully.

"I mean a good old-fashioned English divorce?"

Basil absently sniffed a rose. "I believe, dear chappie, one
makes a start with a firm of private detectives."

"My friend rather wishes to avoid detectives. He wants a
sort of do-it-yourself divorce."

"I don't blame him," Lucy agreed, lighting a cigarette. "Private detectives are utterly ghastly."

"Unfrocked solicitors' clerks with no sense of humor who
suck peppermints," Basil agreed. "My dear wife set them on
me once."

"It's all perfectly simple," said Lucy firmly. "You take a girl to the seaside and you're discovered in a compromising position by the waiter when he brings up the breakfast the next morning."

"You mean that's enough to rev up the machinery of the law?"

"But of course, dear. Lots of my friends strangled with the bonds of matrimony have tried it. You can't imagine the new hats I've had to buy going to court. It's the combination of seaside, waiters, and breakfast," Lucy insisted. "Then the poor dear judge knows where he is. He's probably had a perfectly horrid morning judging whether to hand out decrees, with everyone telling the most frightful fibs. But once he hears the old familiar story he perks up as though he was actually sniffing the ozone. Why, I've heard it dozens of times—'I brought up the coffee and the kippers,' says the waiter, 'and there they were, in a compromising position.' 'Decree *nisi*,' says the judge. "It's as simple as renewing your driving license."

"Personally, I should hate to do anything compromising so early in the morning," murmured Basil, "particularly before I'd had my kippers."

"That's all very well," I pointed out, "but it takes two to make a compromise."

"Naturally, no chappie likes inflicting his future wife with all those waiters and kippers," said Basil briefly, now eyeing me like late-comers in the stalls halfway through the first act.

"But a divorce without a corespondent," Lucy pointed out, "is like a fashionable wedding without a bride."

"I mean, my friend hasn't got a corespondent. He doesn't seem to know any women apart from his wife, and I don't suppose she would do at all. That's why, old lad," I added toward the film star, "I wondered if you happened to know some actress who happened to be out of work at the moment and might take the part?"

Basil raised his eyebrows.

"All perfectly respectable, of course," I went on hastily. "My friend would do the compromising with the utmost decorum."

"I think," said Basil, getting up, "this conversation had better be continued outside."

"Yes, I think so, too." Lucy smiled. "Bye-bye, Gaston. Do come round for a drink soon, won't you? I'd simply love to hear the next act of that divorce."

"Thanks Lucy." I smiled back. "I've got to keep a professional eye on old George, haven't I?"

"As a matter of fact, dear chappie, I do happen to know a girl who rather specializes in such roles," Basil remarked in the corridor.

"Very decent of you to rally round, I must say."

"Always glad to help you or your friends, naturally." Basil paused. "How strange that you should know Lucy Squiffington."

"Lucy's an old chum of my childhood."

"Yes, and a pretty nasty little beast you must have been, by all accounts." Basil laughed. "I don't know how I could go through life myself with the knowledge that I'd once dropped a jellyfish on a lady's tummy."

"We all have our little secrets, don't we Basil?" I reminded him.

"Naturally, dear chappie." Basil suddenly looked solemn, like the time the gasman called a week early. "I might add that I took every opportunity during that ghastly dress rehearsal to impress Lucy what a sterling fellow you were. I praised you to the skies, absolutely. I knew, of course, that you yourself would never go out of your way to burden Lucy with any of my own little immature pranks. Even the greatest of us have tended to be a trifle irresponsible in our youth."

"All right, Basil. I shall never reveal the slugs in your salad days."

"Not that Lucy wouldn't be terribly amused," added the

actor, looking relieved. "We are such very, very close friends. The stage, you know. Such a bond. Now I must go and rehearse," he broke off, reaching the studio door. "There's the little girl's phone number. And I am sure for your part you'll do me a favor by not trying to hobnob with dear Lucy too much? H'm? I am sure it will be for the best, dear chappie. After all, you are not quite—er, in her class, are you? One must simply face these things."

"I have no earthly reason ever to see Lucy again."

"Good," said Basil. "And do remind me, dear chappie when *Saint Joan* comes on, to let you have a couple of free stalls."

Basil went in to rehearse his big mystery serial, which brings the entire nation to a standstill from six-thirty to seven on Tuesdays. I hurried back to my own studio, asking myself if it mattered a hoot whether I saw Lucy again in my life. Particularly as our income brackets were as wide apart as the Bank of England and the local slate club. Lucy was merely another female in my social life, I decided, like Connie or Mrs. Hildenborough. After all, I told myself, I was a lucky chap. I was still firmly engaged to quite the nicest girl in the whole world.

Chapter Fifteen

"The train standing at number fifteen platform," announced the loud-speaker, "is the two thirty-five to Whortleton-on-Sea. Please form an orderly queue and do not rush the ticket barrier."

"That's us," I said to Miles.

"Eh? What?"

"Our train. We join the end of the queue behind the kid with the bucket being sick over the policeman."

"This is incredible," muttered Miles.

"For heaven's sake, man, cheer up! You're supposed to be ruddy Casanova, not Marley's ghost."

"It's only that I imagined the business wouldn't be quite so public as this," Miles added miserably. "It always seems much simpler in the newspapers."

My cousin was standing beside me under the clock, in his holiday tweeds and dark glasses, clutching his brief case. All round us surged the normal activity of Victoria station on a hot Saturday afternoon in July.

There's nowhere on earth more wonderful than England in summertime—if the sun happens to shine—with the long evenings, the strawberries and cream, the sweet peas, the lazy rivers, the smell of new-mown grass, and the dozy afternoons ticking softly away with the click of bat on ball. For all the isles of Bermuda, Honolulu, or Tahiti I'll settle for this sceptered one, even though it is largely uninhabitable between Guy Fawkes Night and the Boat Race. And admittedly when the season does arrive to enjoy the silver sea this precious stone is set in, there's an awful lot of the happy breed of men to share it with.

"Sure you still want to go?" I asked Miles, as somebody walked over his foot.

He gave a determined nod. "Decidedly. Besides, I have already bought the tickets."

We started to push our way across the sea-going current toward platform fifteen.

"I suppose she's going to turn up at the hotel?" muttered Miles. "Thank heavens I decided against our making the journey together."

"Absolutely guaranteed it. Seems a reliable type, too. Fully experienced."

"I should hate to think all this effort completely wasted."

"So should I," I agreed warmly. "Watch out for that porter practising tank tactics with his luggage truck."

Miles licked his lips. "You know, Gaston, it's—it's very decent of you to go to all this trouble."

"Always ready to help one of the family."

"I know we have perhaps had our little differences in the past," he conceded, as somebody caught him in the middle with a cricket bat.

"Clash of cousinly temperaments. Very common. Gave Shakespeare half his plots."

"But I'd like to say how much I appreciate your doing all this for me."

"No trouble at all," I told him. "Mind that kid with the yacht. I diagnose him as a case of incipient vomiting, too."

I hadn't done all that for Miles, of course. I'd done it for Connie.

"I've brought round Miles's woolly slippers," she had said,

when I found her on the mat after that episode of "Ambulance Entrance" had been safely taped. "He seemed to have forgotten them. And his poor feet do get so cold at night."

"I hope you haven't been waiting long?" I asked, letting her into the empty flat. "I also hope," I added, "you know Miles is planning to go ahead and help himself to a divorce?"

"Yes." Connie felt for her handkerchief. "He sent me a letter. Twenty pages, some of it very, very lovely indeed. Quite poetic."

"But dash it, Connie! Surely you're not going to let this fooling go any further?"

"I shall not stand in his way, Gaston." Connie took on the air of a steadfast martyr offered pen and ink at the stake. "I know my duty. Miles has a great future, and young Bartholomew and I are mere encumbrances. How proud I shall be, as I hold up my child in my arms, to catch a glimpse of him riding past in his robes to take his seat as a life peer in the House of Lords."

I fancied Connie had an enthusiastic view of the procedure, but merely suggested it would be nice for Miles to have her at home to polish his coronet in the evenings.

"Do you think I should tell young Bartholomew all?" asked Connie.

"I fancy that would only confuse the issue." I laughed.

But I don't think she was in the mood to see it.

"Young Bartholomew and I shall start a new life." Connie dabbed her eyes. "We shall manage somehow. It will be best for Miles if we spend the rest of our days in exile. In St. Moritz or Cannes, or somewhere."

"You know Miles has actually asked me to tee up the divorce for him? Not, of course, that I want to be his ruddy caddy in your twosome."

"I only ask, Gaston, that you do all in your power to smooth the way for us."

"Look—why don't you nip down to Lincoln's Inn and see one of those slick lawyer chaps? They extract divorces from the courts like dentists extracting teeth. All perfectly painless, and no complications once the numb feeling has worn off."

"I'd much rather you did as Miles wanted, Gaston." She laid her head on my shoulder. "Please . . . for my sake."

"Oh, all right," I said.

I rather absent-mindedly patted her hand.

"Besides," she added, nestling up a bit. "Miles was absolutely horrid to a very nice friend of mine in that night club. Do you think St. Moritz would really be the right place for my exile? Or should I try somewhere like Jamaica or Rio instead?"

Connie had hardly left before Miles appeared, announcing he'd saved up a whole twelve hundred calories for his dinner.

"Your missus must have dropped your woolly slippers on the mat," I told him, putting on my little apron to grill his steak. "And you'll be glad to know I've got someone lined up for you to do your compromising with."

"Excellent!" Miles rubbed his hands. "I've had hardly a moment to give thought to the matter today, dashing round the docks looking for Mr. Odysseus. He seems a most elusive gentleman. I suppose I shall have to pay this compromsing woman handsomely? How much will be adequate? Three hundred pounds? Four hundred? Five?"

If I'd known that Miles had five hundred quid lying about I'd have already suggested a bit down for board and lodging. But I merely said I would give her a ring and ask the fees in her private practice.

"It'll cost you quite a bit, darling," said Dolores, when I called to see her. "Plus expenses, of course," she added, shifting a pair of Sealyhams that were growling at some Scotties.

"Naturally." I moved uneasily away from a parrot who was eyeing me suspiciously. "You will find the gentleman for whom

I am acting perfectly reasonable about terms. To the point of generosity."

"Of course, I wouldn't do it for anyone except a friend of Basil Beauchamp's." We edged discreetly among the hamsters. "Are you really a friend of Basil's? No funny business, mind you."

"Of course I am," I pointed out. "I could hardly have found you here otherwise, could I?"

Dolores, who turned out to be a dark, emaciated-looking girl in a mauve overall, worked in the Pet Boutique in Bond Street.

"Not that I've seen Basil for simply ages." She sorted out a pile of puppies. "Isn't he a darling man? I met him when I was an extra in the studio, during *St. George and the Dragon*. He looked absolutely divine in a visor."

"Quite. Now—er, how about the lolly?"

She sprinkled ants' eggs into a bowl of goldfish. "It depends what you want, dear."

"Just—well, a decent compromise, that's all," I returned, beginning to feel rather lost.

"I mean, does your gentleman want me in bed or out? It's extra in bed, of course."

"Naturally. I think he'd be glad enough to have you up and about."

"I could do it for fifty keeping all my things on. It's a hundred in my slip, a hundred and twenty-five showing my legs, a hundred and fifty showing my—"

"We'll have the hundred quid one," I interrupted, feeling this the best value in the tariff.

"Of course, dear, if your gentleman really wanted to go the limit—"

"Exactly. When can we fix a date for the operation?" I asked quickly.

"Not till next month, darling."

"Next month?" I remembered Miles's holiday would be up. "Couldn't you manage to squeeze in a day, or rather a night, before then?"

"But darling, I don't see how I possibly can. Not till I start my own holidays. We're utterly overwhelmed this time of the year, and I always help out Miss Treadburn—she's the boss, a complete darling—with the summer kenneling. Absolutely everyone is going out of town just now and leaving their pets. You'd never believe what I've had in my flat—a pair of Alsatians, six budgereegahs, and a monkey, not to mention the fish. And then there's the poodle-clipping. 'Dolores,' Miss Treadburn said to me only yesterday, 'for poodle-clipping there's no one to touch you in London.' So I said—"

"I expect we can fix up some time convenient for you and the animals," I hazarded, though feeling rather doubtful.

"I expect we can, darling. Give me another ring. Oh, and don't make it Brighton, will you, darling? A girl can always do with a change."

"Fixing up your corespondent was pretty easy," I reflected to Miles some time later, when he was already coming up for his second turn on the divan. "It's the theater of operations that presents the difficulty. Why the devil do you want to get a divorce in July, particularly when it looks as though we're in for a heat wave? It's absolutely ruddy impossible to book a double room at the seaside anywhere. At least, in a hotel where they have waiters to bring up the breakfast."

"We shall need a single room as well, of course."

"What on earth for?" I was becoming rather testy with the chap. "You're not asking our old grandma along for sea-water treatment of the back or anything, are you?"

"You will be accompanying me, naturally," announced Miles calmly. "You don't imagine I intend to suffer this extremely unusual and somewhat alarming experience by myself, do you?"

"Me? I am most definitely not going to play gooseberry."

"I have the final execution of the plan carefully worked out," Miles continued, taking no notice. "The corespondent will sleep in the single room, while you and I share the double. In the morning, the kippers already being ordered, you and she will rapidly change places. As soon as the waiter has left, you may return and enjoy your breakfast." He gave one of his smiles. "You see, Gaston, I am not devoid of guile when necessary. It is simply that I usually manage to conceal it beneath my engagingly frank exterior. You will now continue to ring round all the seaside hotels in the Automobile Association handbook. Only the four-star ones, of course."

That was typical of my cousin, imagining he could cast off the bonds of matrimony like a dirty shirt and then leaving all the work to me. But the trouble with modern Britain, whether it's hotels or hospitals, is too many people chasing too few beds. The hotels kept regretting they were booked to the eaves. I started to feel that Miles, Dolores, and myself would end up with a jolly night of it on the rocks at Land's End.

Then I had a terrific stroke of luck.

Chapter Sixteen

"Sir Lancelot Spratt's lipstick," I announced, "is a trifle on the thick side. Though he could do with a touch more eye shadow."

"How about his powder, Dr. Grimsdyke?"

"A dab or two, I'd say."

The pretty girl in the pink overall ran her puff over the surgeon's forehead.

"Grimsdyke," said Sir Lancelot.

"Sir?"

"Is it not a frightening reflection on our age that every evening not only consultant surgeons but bishops, barristers, businessmen, and backbenchers sit back and let themselves be made up like one of the girls from Madame Tellier's?"

"Oh, I don't know, sir."

"I wonder," growled Sir Lancelot, "what Mr. Gladstone would have said."

It hadn't been half as tough as I expected, persuading the old boy to go on the telly. I suppose with the fishing season half over he was keen to raise public support for his idea of a teen-agers readjustment center. Though I must say, he didn't seem quite so keen, now he sat glaring at himself in that bright bulb-fringed mirror they have up in the studio makeup department.

"Not nervous, I hope, sir?" I jollied him along.

"Exceedingly. Unlike that blunted battle-ax Dame Hilda—I beg your pardon, Grimsdyke, I quite overlooked for the moment your impending relationship—unlike Dame Hilda I am not accustomed to making regular exhibitions of myself in public. However, our views differ so greatly I should be lacking moral strength if I declined to cross swords with her whenever the occasion demands."

I nodded. "As you're on the air in ten minutes, sir, I'd better get down to the studio. The hospitality room's at the end of the corridor," I added, remembering that even the bishops like to drop in for a quick spot of hospitality before facing the cameras.

"Thank you, Grimsdyke. You have some flair as an anesthetist."

The studio, like all television studios before transmission, resembled the Black Hole of Calcutta wired for electronics. It was all cameras and cables and men in frayed khaki pull-overs. Among them stumbled the studio manager, with a rapt and vacant look on his face and his own walkie-talkie, through which he was receiving messages from on high, like Joan of Arc.

I'd already lunched that day with Dame Hilda—she brought me some very nice messages from Anemone—and I knew she was as much at ease as Pavlova having another bash at *Swan Lake*. But poor Sir Lancelot, settled on one of those hard chairs they give people to squirm in during television interviews, simply stared in alarm at the monitor set, showing a couple of sporty seals tossing balls to each other.

"Two minutes, everyone," called the studio manager, getting the call from above.

Sir Lancelot's face went blank, like the monitor screen.

"I intend to be *quite* merciless toward you, Sir Lancelot." Dame Hilda smiled, shaking a finger. "Nor do I expect you to pull any punches with me. All's fair in war and television, you know."

Sir Lancelot's face took on a confused jagged look, like the monitor. I stood quietly in the background. Personally, if Evan Crippen had wanted to interview me, I should have gone abroad, grown a beard, and changed my name. As I waited for the red light and watched the girl who did the announcing adjusting her television neckline, I could only feel acutely sorry for the old boy.

"Ten seconds," said the studio manager.

The red light went up, and the one-thousand-and fifty-fourth edition of "This Evening" took the air.

The program started off as usual, with a chap holding forth about the political situation, a girl explaining how she made bedspreads from old typewriter ribbons, another girl singing a witty little song, and then another chap holding forth about something else. Finally, the light flashed on Sir Lancelot's camera, and Evan Crippen started introducing them to God knows how many millions sitting agog over their high tea or cocktails, according to taste.

"Sir Lancelot—" Evan Crippen turned on the surgeon. "You wrote recently in the press that far too much fuss is made over the problems of the modern teen-ager?"

"Well, I—"

"You seriously mean that this, probably the greatest social question of our country, is receiving not too little but far too much public attention?"

"I hardly said—"

"Sir Lancelot, I am utterly surprised that a man of your standing—particularly in the great profession of medicine—should take such a miserably mean attitude."

"I assure you that I—"

"Many teen-agers are watching this program, and I need hardly tell you their reaction. I am appalled at your harsh Victorian approach to the problem of these delicate saplings growing in the mysterious forest of adulthood," ended Evan Crippen, seeming rather pleased with the remark.

"Let me tell you that—"

"Sir Lancelot, would you regard yourself as a square?"

"Would I regard myself as a *what?*"

"Thank you, Sir Lancelot. I am sure that was very enlightening. Dame Hilda—" He swiveled the sanitary-inspector's nose. "You are, of course, our greatest national authority on juvenile delinquency?"

Dame Hilda smiled.

"I believe I am admitted to be."

"Quite. Dame Hilda, I have here a cutting from a local paper of some years ago. Will you explain to the viewers, if you please, how you were once convicted in a magistrate's court and fined five pounds for stealing a hat from a milliner's shop?"

Dame Hilda gave a gasp, and so did everyone else in the studio. "But . . . but . . . that was so long ago."

"Quite so. But it *was* shoplifting."

"I . . . I was a mere girl at the time . . . and it was such a pretty hat . . . I don't know for the life of me what came over . . ."

"Go on, Dame Hilda."

"Oh, dear!" Dame Hilda produced a handkerchief. "I thought everyone had forgotten . . . it's terrible after all these years . . ."

Evan Crippen smiled. "Go on, Dame Hilda, if you please."

Sir Lancelot tapped him on the shoulder. "Just a minute, sonny."

"Would you mind!" snapped the interviewer.

"Do you know what I think of you?" growled Sir Lancelot, taking him by the lapel. "I think you have the mentality of a nasty-minded youth prowling round suburban back gardens at night, in the hope of espying through some uncurtained window the sight of a respectable housewife standing in her underclothes."

"Really!" cried Evan Crippen.

"Furthermore," continued Sir Lancelot, taking the other lapel, "you have the manners of a school bully, the gallantry of a Soho pimp, the compassion of a Barbary slave driver, and about as much tact as an elephant reversing into a greenhouse."

"Let me go at once! The viewers—"

"Do you know what I should like to do with you?" Sir Lancelot shook him a bit. "I should like to take you down to St. Swithin's Hospital and lock you for the night in the mortuary. Then you might begin to see we are all feeble human beings made of the same flesh and blood, even though our egos sometimes become inflated like toy balloons."

"If you do not take your hands off me instantly—!"

"Let me give you a little advice, sonny. If you wish to continue making fools of people through this contraption you are perfectly at liberty to do so. I would only counsel you to read the Fables of Aesop, with particular attention to the Ass in the Lion's Skin, and a side glance at the Fox and the Sour Grapes. You will now kindly apologize to the lady."

"This program never apologizes to anybody," snapped Evan Crippen.

"In that case, I shall break your ruddy neck."

"Oh, Sir Lancelot!" cried Dame Hilda, falling into his arms.

"Cut!" cried the studio manager. "We're running that film of village life instead."

"I'll have you thrown out of here!" stormed Evan Crippen, pointing a finger in my direction. "Has everyone gone mad?"

"Wonderful program," said the producer through the intercom. "Pure television."

"I want a drink," said Sir Lancelot.

"So do I," I told him.

I hustled the two performers out of the studio. I pushed them into the local round the back. I bought Dame Hilda a large brandy. She drank it gazing up at Sir Lancelot like one of her own ruddy teen-agers stuck in the studio lift with the latest pop singer.

"My dear lady." Sir Lancelot wiped off his makeup with one hand and took hers in the other. "I trust you are not too distressed?"

"But Sir Lancelot! That dreadful man! You were so wonderful."

"I hope, madam, I shall never stand idly by to witness a lady being humiliated by a cad."

"And that dreadful revelation!"

"I can assure you, madam, my own cupboard contains many interesting pieces of osteology."

"Surely you can no longer think anything of me?"

"On the contrary, I think a great deal more of you."

"But you must call me Hilda."

"But I should be delighted."

"Sir Lancelot, you were so forceful . . . so strong. A true knight, in shining armor."

"Another brandy, Hilda?"

"Thank you. How often have I suspected a beard indicated inner strength!"

"That is kind of you, Hilda."

"A beard does not lend a man character. It expresses it."

"A charitable observation."

"You must, in your youth, have been such an athletic man."

"I did indeed enjoy some success at putting the shot."

I began to feel rather out of this.

"Now Sir Lancelot, I must do everything in my power to help your new scheme down in Wales. Perhaps I could bring over a party of London girls for a fortnight's holiday? I could easily arrange for you to receive a most generous grant for their maintenance, and it would be a fine beginning for your clinic."

"Excellent, Hilda! Why not next weekend?"

"Of course. Next weekend—" Dame Hilda caught sight of me. "But next Saturday I am due to begin my own summer holiday with Anemone and Gaston at Whortleton."

"Ah, tut," said Sir Lancelot.

"And of course Gaston and Anemone couldn't possibly go down to Whortleton alone. That wouldn't be at all nice."

"Look here, Dame Hilda," I suggested quickly. "Why don't you, I and Anemone all start on the Monday, instead? I mean, Monday's a far better day to begin a trip to the seaside. Much more room in the sea, and the pierrots will be all fresh with a new show."

"If you really wouldn't mind, Gaston—" said Dame Hilda doubtfully.

"Not a bit. I mean, really, I'm terribly disappointed. But I'm sure Sir Lancelot needs a little of your time too, Dame Hilda," I added, with a bit of a smirk.

"In that case, I will alter the hotel reservations."

"Don't you worry, Dame Hilda. I'll attend to that."

"But I could easily send them a wire—"

"No bother at all," I told her. "I'll pick up the phone just as soon as I get back to my flat."

I didn't, of course. I left Sir Lancelot to take Dame Hilda out to dinner, and nipped back to find my cousin. And that was why Miles and myself, that Saturday afternoon, were in a compartment with about two dozen other people, all going to Whortleton.

Chapter Seventeen

"What on earth do you suppose has happened to that blasted woman?" demanded Miles. "Damnation! I'm absolutely certain she's never going to turn up at all."

"Give her a chance, old lad." I tried to placate him. "After all, it's hardly past 10 P.M."

"It's all your fault," returned Miles shortly.

"My fault?"

"Yes, you've told her the wrong date, time, hotel, and seaside resort, I shouldn't wonder. You always were absolutely hopeless trying to organize anything, even the jam cupboard at school."

"That's a bit hard, I must say! I've gone to all this ruddy trouble, just because you want to kick out Connie like a cold hot-water bottle. And I've still got to tell Anemone and Dame Hilda no end of fibs on Monday about you and your wife taking over their room for the night. Not to mention what I shall say when the sordid truth comes out in the divorce court. Except that," I reflected, "I shall, of course, be nicely married by then."

Miles continued to pace angrily up and down our bedroom in the Surfview Hotel.

The Surfview at Whortleton, like the pier and the railway, had been built for the pleasure of our Victorian ancestors, when they decided there was nothing like sea air to cure everything from the green sickness to the galloping scrofula—and, poor chaps, they hadn't much else to try with. Life at Whortleton had centered mainly round the lobster pots until these ancestors started trundling up and down the beach in their bathing machines, exclaiming that nothing was quite so healthy as the tang of the ozone, though actually it's only the smell of rotting seaweed and the local sewage. The management of the Surfview, having hit on just the right décor to keep the ancestors happy between dips, hadn't seen much reason to change it since, and our room contained a couple of beds with brass knobs, a wardrobe hefty enough to resist armor-piercing shells, a curly stand for your hats and umbrellas, a picture of a stag rather puzzled to find itself on a mountain peak, and a framed notice explaining that if anyone swiped your valuables while in residence it was jolly well your own fault.

"I'm sorry," muttered Miles, kicking the commode. "I'm somewhat worked up, that's all. You can hardly blame me."

"Perfectly understandable," I agreed sportingly. "Let's go straight down and have another recce. for Dolores. Besides," I added, remembering, "we've got to organize those kippers. There'd be no point in the outing at all if the three of us found ourselves picking the bones out of our teeth downstairs in the dining room."

"You go." Miles reached for his brief case. "I have some essential lecture notes to prepare. Don't forget I start again at St. Swithin's on Monday morning."

"You might also have a dummy run at your compromising position," I suggested. "You could practise on the hat stand."

Miles raised his eyebrows. "I shall be observed with my jacket off. I presume that will be enough?"

"Well—I'd throw in your collar and shoes for good measure."

As Miles only grunted I went down to the hall and looked

hopefully for Dolores among the palms. There was no one in sight at all, except a thin, gray-haired, solemn-looking chap in library glasses picking his teeth behind a desk at the door, whom I gathered was the night porter.

"I suppose there are still plenty of trains from London?" I asked him, strolling up in a casual way.

"Last one arrives on Saturdays at ten-ten, sir. Except for the three o'clock, of course."

"Oh." I looked at my watch. "I expect Mrs. Grimsdyke will arrive on that ten-ten. Perhaps you would kindly show her up to Mr. Miles Grimsdyke's room, number six?"

"Certainly, sir."

"Now, about breakfast."

"Ah, yes, sir."

The porter gravely opened his book.

"Kippers for one, for me, in number ten. Double kippers for Mr. Miles Grimsdyke and this ruddy—Mrs. Grimsdyke, in number six."

"Very good, sir."

"Good lord—" I felt a wave of alarm. "The waiter will actually bring the kippers in, won't he? I mean, he won't just leave them on the mat? That is, you follow me, they might get cold, mightn't they? And there's nothing nastier than a cold kipper, is there?"

"If you would prefer, sir, I shall serve the breakfasts myself."

"Would you?" I took a good look at the chap. "Yes, I think that would be just the ticket. I suppose," I added, very cunningly, "you wear glasses only for reading?"

"Yes, sir. The doctor tells me I suffer from a degree of myopia, sir."

"Excellent! Long sight perfect, I take it? And I expect you're an observant sort of chap—I mean, in a hotel, with things going on all round, you have to be, don't you?"

"My hobby in the afternoons is bird watching, sir."

"That's absolutely capital. And you must have a pretty sharp memory for faces?"

"That is essential in my job, sir."

"I thought so. Good. Well. Perhaps you'll see that Mr. Miles Grimsdyke has a good breakfast tomorrow morning?" I slipped the chap a quid. "Extremely keen on his breakfast, Mr. Miles Grimsdyke."

"That is very kind of you, sir. You are one of Lynx's new men, I take it, sir?"

"One of—one of what?"

"The Lynx Detective Agency, sir. They generally use us. I said to the manager only the other day, sir," he added with a fatherly smile, "we might as well put their sign outside along with the A.A. and the R.A.C., sir."

"What on earth do you mean?"

I stared at him indignantly, though taking my hat off to the chap for rumbling my little scheme.

"Oh, come, sir." The porter gave another paternal smirk. "Honeymoons and divorces, you can spot them a mile off. Not that we get anything like the divorce trade we used to, sir. I remember the days—it's long ago now—when some week-ends you couldn't get in the Snuggery Bar for detectives. They don't seem to go in for that style of divorce any more, sir. Different class of people taken it up, I suppose. You see it everywhere. Times change. Mind you, I like to see a divorce done proper, with dignity. If I had my way there'd be a little ceremony in the court, with the judge passing back the bride to her father and the detective at the husband's side to pocket the ring—"

"All right," I interrupted. "I might as well be perfectly frank and confess what we're up to. But if the blasted corespondent doesn't turn up we'll just have to scratch the fixture and arrange a replay later, won't we?"

"Don't lose heart, sir. There's still time yet, and some of these ladies are extremely busy in the evenings, sir."

I pottered round the lounge, looking at my watch. I turned over the magazines and stared at those booklets putting overseas holiday-makers right about Britain, all timbered inns and groaning boards and jolly landlords quaffing it round the dear old stocks. But by ten-thirty I began to feel dully that Dolores was definitely a nonrunner.

"I'm going to have a mooch round outside," I told the porter. "If a skinny brunette called Dolores shows up, deliver her to number six, with my compliments."

Being Saturday, the night life of Whortleton was reaching its weekly climax. The therapeutic charms of the place had now been rather ousted by other attractions, and all round were establishments dripping with fairy lights providing everything necessary for a happy seaside holiday—rock, fish teas, funny hats, rude post cards, jellied eels, dodgem cars, insecticides, and palmists. I wandered among the crowds on the prom, and, buying a bag of shrimps, absently peeled a few leaning against the rail. I felt like Napoleon when the guards cut and ran at Waterloo. All that trouble and nothing to show for it, I reflected moodily, except Miles enjoying an extra kipper for his breakfast.

"Damn Dolores," I muttered into the shrimps. "I should have known better than bank on one of Basil's ruddy camp followers."

I turned to stare out to sea for inspiration.

"By jove—!"

The end of the pier announced in colored lights:

THE WHORTLETON PIERROTS
SPECIAL ATTRACTION
THIS WEEK—FAMOUS TV STARS
THE JELLYBONE SISTERS

Five minutes later I was in Gertie's dressing room.

"Why, hello, Doctor!" she exclaimed, putting down her Guinness. "This is a surprise, and no mistake."

"Gertrude," I said earnestly, without wasting time. "I have a rather peculiar request to make of you."

Chapter Eighteen

∽

"My dear old lad, I really can't see what you're complaining about," I protested to Miles, after explaining the change of cast. "You ought to feel jolly glad that Gertie has agreed to help out, after finishing one extremely exhausting performance on the pier. And I might tell you, she's only coming as a personal favor to me. Though of course," I added, "you'll have to cough up another hundred quid as well."

"It all seems very irregular," muttered Miles.

"The whole business is hardly the model of a conventional evening."

"I mean this—this Dolores was a professional. She knew what she was doing. Now we are simply placing ourselves in the hands of an unqualified practitioner."

"You've nothing whatever to worry about," I assured the idiot. "I've explained the drill, and an old trouper like Gertie would certainly never let you down. Think of it this way," I went on. "All that sweetness you're spreading with your hundred quid—a nice little nest egg for the poor dear when her ligaments finally calcify and the terrible morning arrives when she finds she can no longer pick up her handkerchief with her teeth backwards. She'll remember you with gratitude for years and years, and probably embroider you little presents for Christmas."

Miles groaned. "To think! I am obliged to spend the night with a female contortionist. It really is too much."

I was about to point out he was only obliged to have breakfast with a female contortionist, when a knock came on the door.

"Yes?"

The gray-haired night porter appeared.

"Mrs. Grimsdyke, sir," he announced solemnly.

"Why, hello," said Gertie, standing in the doorway and staring at both of us, rather like the stag in the picture.

"Say something in front of the porter," I muttered to Miles. "She's supposed to be your loving wife, not the char come to do the floors."

"Er—good evening, my dear," said Miles. "How are you, my dear? I trust you are well, my dear? Don't you think we are having excellent weather, my dear? Though perhaps somewhat chilly in the evenings for this time of the year, my dear?" He licked his lips, seeming to have come to the end of his love talk. "Perhaps you would care for some refreshment, my dear?"

"Thanks ever so, I'd love a Guinness." Gertie smiled, looking relieved.

"One Guinness," I told the porter.

"Very good, sir. If I may say so, sir, that was a very useful little speech of your client's, sir. Fair sticks in the memory, that does, sir."

"Thank you, porter."

"I am glad, sir, to see we are setting about your new position in the proper way."

"Very kind of you, porter."

"I feel, sir, we shall in time get quite to the top of our tree, sir."

"Get that fool out of here," muttered Miles.

"One Guinness," I repeated.

"Certainly, sir."

"Well," said Gertie, taking off her hat as the door shut.

"It is extremely kind of you to agree to take part in these somewhat distasteful proceedings," began Miles at once.

"Distasteful?" Gertie threw me a glance. "I hope there's going to be nothing distasteful about it, I must say."

"I mean, these somewhat degrading proceedings."

"Well, I like that! I'm not going to degrade myself for anybody, let me tell you for a start. I've been top of the bill now for longer than I'd like to—"

"What I mean, madam," interrupted Miles, "is that I don't do this sort of thing every night."

"Oh? And I do, I suppose?"

"No, no, of course you don't! I am only trying to explain it is an extremely unusual situation for me."

"And what do you suppose it is for me, may I ask?"

"Gaston, you will kindly entertain the lady." Miles sat abruptly at the dressing table. "I have my notes to complete."

There was another knock on the door.

"Your Guinness, madam."

"Oh, ta," said Gertie, brightening up again.

"Will there be anything more, sir?"

"Not at all. You can leave me to run the show till breakfast."

"I'm *sure* I can, sir. Good night, sir. Good night, all."

"Good night."

My cousin sat with his back to us, silently writing his notes. Gertie curled on the bed and drank her Guinness. I leant against the commode and tried to make light conversation. By eleven-thirty I felt it was high time for the redeployment of forces.

"You take your little case and toddle along to number ten," I told Gertie. "I'll set my alarm for seven, then creep down the passage and give you a call. You simply put on your dressing gown and we'll do a quick switch. Once the kippers are served, you can nip back to number ten and eat your own in peace."

Gertie looked doubtful.

"I hope there isn't going to be any monkey business."

"Monkey business? Good lord, of course not."

"I know that type," she added, nodding toward Miles.

"Oh, he's perfectly harmless," I assured her. "He's just a little edgy at the moment."

"I'm not so sure I fancy being all alone with him, that's straight."

"But the porter with the kippers will be there to chaperone you," I pointed out.

"I still don't like it. I had a nasty experience once at Hastings."

"It would be best if the lady now left us for her own apartments," said Miles wearily, getting up.

"Okey-doke, dearie." Gertie got off the bed. "No offense intended, I'm sure, as long as you're a good boy."

There was a knock on the door.

"What on earth—?" I murmured.

The porter appeared.

"Mrs. Grimsdyke," he announced.

"Why, it's Cissy," exclaimed Gertie, as her sister walked in. "How nice of you to call."

"Oh, Gert," cried her sister. "Are you all right? I've been worrying myself proper stiff ever since you left the digs. I said to myself, I'd never forgive myself if anything happened to Gert, I wouldn't, not after I'd told her to have a go. Though of course, we can all do with the lolly, can't we? I mean to say, we know the doctor here's a proper gentleman. But we don't know if it goes for his friend, do we? Remember what happened in Hastings? With people these days you never can tell—"

"Another Guinness," I told the porter briefly.

"Very good, sir. If I may say so, sir, I think we are quite right having a second string to our bow. With the courts these days we never can tell, sir."

"Thank you, porter. That Guinness, please."

"At once, sir."

"What in the name of the devil's all this?" demanded Miles, starting to jump about rather.

"That's him, is it?" asked Cissy, inspecting my cousin doubtfully.

"My sister Cissy," Gertie introduced her. "She's a proper miracle on the parallel bars."

"Anyway, I said to myself," Cissy went on, not seeming to find Miles worth further attention, "if Gertie wants to get out of it I'm game to try—after all, a hundred pounds is a hundred pounds, especially these hard times—so I remembered the name was the same as the doctor's and said I was Mrs. just in case."

"Stop it!" barked Miles.

"Coo, listen to him!" exclaimed the sisters, with pained glances.

"I said stop it," repeated Miles angrily. "This foolishness cannot be allowed to continue. Gaston! Do something! At once. One of these women will have to go."

"Did you hear that?" demanded Gertie indignantly.

"He called us women," agreed Cissy.

"Well, I never."

"In our profession we're accustomed to being addressed as ladies, thank you."

"Cheek, if you ask me."

"Oh, God," muttered Miles.

"Look here, Gertie," I chipped in. "We can get this sorted out in no time. After all, you're only doing the performance as a favor to me, aren't you? Neither of you need give a hoot about this chap, and if he has got rather nasty manners and worse intentions you'll never have to set eyes on him once you've got his cash in your handbags."

"That's true, dearie," both girls conceded, very fairly.

"Now let's decide quickly which one of you is going to stay for breakfast. Then she can retire to her own room straight away and lock the door. And pile all the furniture up against it, too, if she feels like it."

"I'll do it, Gert," said Cissy.

"No, I'll do it," insisted Gertie. "You never did like sleeping in strange beds."

"Good," I agreed smartly. "Gertie gets the part. Now if you, Cissy, will kindly make your way home—"

There was a knock on the door.

"That'll be your Guinness," I said.

The porter appeared.

"Mrs. Grimsdyke," he announced.

"You'd better make it three Guinnesses," I told him.

"Why, Joan! Isn't that nice?" said the two Jellybone Sisters. "Come in, dearie, and sit down."

"If there's any room," I added.

"No, sir," said the porter, shaking his head from the doorway. "I am disappointed, sir. Frankly, we are overdoing it, sir. Two ladies lends a little variety and added interest to the subsequent proceedings. But three would simply make a nasty crowd in the witness box, sir."

"The Guinness," I reminded him.

"Immediately, sir."

"Gaston," hissed Miles. "Gaston—get these females out of here. All of them. I intend to return home instantly."

"Oo, so you're the dirty old man, are you?" said Joan, giving Miles a wink. "Well, I never. You meet all kinds at the seaside, don't you? I thought of you and Cissy all alone in this hotbed," she went on earnestly to her sisters, "and it made me go all queer inside. I said to myself, even if Cissy and me did win when we tossed for it, I'll come along and do the dirty work all the same. And anyway, everyone says the beds here are that damp it's a wonder you don't find seaweed growing in them, and that would never do with your rheumatism, Gertie, especially as we've got the show to think about. So I said—"

"Get out!" shouted Miles suddenly. "I—I mean if you ladies would be so kind as to . . . to . . . to . . ."

He sank onto the bed, holding his head.

"Feeling poorly, dearie?" asked Gertie solicitously.

"He's had a turn," observed Cissy.

"Just a bit of nervous strain," I explained, hastily filling a glass with water.

"Of course I was forgetting, you're a doctor," said Joan. "The poor thing! Is he going to be all right?"

"Here, let me undo his collar," suggested Gertie.

"Lie him down here, Doctor, and I'll put some of my cologne on his temples," added Cissy, opening her handbag.

"Do you think if we did a bit of our act it might cheer him up?" asked Gertie.

"That's it, girls." Joan got on the floor. "Let's show him the reverse handstand pyramid."

I splashed water in Miles's face. The girls did the reverse handstand pyramid. I fanned him with the hand towel. As the girls switched to scratching the backs of their necks with their toes I finally got Miles sitting up, looking rather pale.

"Don't worry, old lad," I muttered, now feeling thoroughly sorry for the poor chap. "Give me half a jiffy and I'll have all this straightened out."

"Gaston . . . you've got to get rid of these . . . these . . . refugees from the Wolfenden Report. You've got to get rid of them at once," was all he could mutter.

"Ladies," I announced to the Jellybone Sisters. "We think your act's absolutely terrific, but my friend here has changed his mind about the evening."

"Changed his mind?" Gertie glanced up from between her heels.

"Yes. He's decided he's not going on with the divorce proceedings any longer."

"Oh, what a shame," said Cissy.

"He'll pay the fee, naturally," I added hastily. "But for the moment he wants to be alone, until he feels a bit stronger."

There was a knock on the door.

"What on earth—"

The porter appeared.

"Mrs. Grimsdyke," he announced.

In strode Dolores, with a mastiff.

"Another Guinness," I said briskly.

"Certainly, sir. And—I regret to say so, sir—this is taking sledgehammers to crack nuts good and proper, sir."

"Who on earth are all these people?" exclaimed Dolores.

"Sort of cabaret act. To pass the evening. No telly here, you know. That's my friend," I added. "The pale chap on the bed."

"What a lovely doggie," said the Jellybone Sisters, untangling themselves and patting the thing.

"And where the devil did you get to, may I ask?" I demanded, eyeing Dolores pretty severely.

"Darling, it was hell in the kennels today. I'd never have made it at all if Miss Treadburn hadn't given me a lift in her car. As it is, I had to bring one of the boarders with me. You'd never imagine the crush this weekend, with absolutely everyone going on their holiday. We even had an alligator, if you please."

"Quite," I interrupted, feeling it was urgent to cut down the establishment of corespondents a bit. "Thank you, ladies," I told the Jellybone Sisters, who seemed to have finished the midnight matinée. "You've been very sweet, and if you'd now be kind enough to push off once my friend here has written you a check—"

"Yes, of course, check," mumbled Miles, feeling for his pen.

"I must say, I didn't expect a party," observed Dolores. "It's a bit unusual, but I'm for anything to break the monotony. Dingo, don't bite the gentleman." The dog was sniffing Miles, though he didn't look to me particularly appetizing at the moment. "Where do you want me to sleep?" she added, slipping off her coat.

"We'll go into that when I've cleared the stage for the next scene."

"Oh, very well, darling. You know best. Have you got a cigarette? I'm simply dying for one."

"In a second, damn it!" I told her testily, trying to help Miles write the check. "Just as soon as we're alone."

There was a knock on the door.

"Mrs. Grimsdyke," announced the porter resignedly.

"Then you'd better make it five Guinnesses," I explained. "Oh, hello," was all I could think of adding, with a stupid sort of grin. "You don't care much for Guinness, Connie, do you?"

Chapter Nineteen

"Perhaps I intrude?" began Connie.

"Darling!" Miles came to life. "My beloved! My heart's ease! My angel pie! Have you the car? Take me back home instantly."

"That's exactly why I came down," Connie added calmly. "Though I didn't expect to find myself so heavily outnumbered."

Connie's arrival, naturally, raised even more interest than the dog's. The Jellybone Sisters stood in a group and giggled. Dolores gave her a long look and announced, "Won't *anyone* give me a cigarette?" The mastiff itself started growling at Miles's sponge bag. I leaned against the hatstand, and I could only feel thankful that at least we seemed to have come to the end of our visiting list.

"I didn't know you were intending to settle in the East, Miles," Connie continued dryly. "You know how the heat upsets you so."

"East? Me? What east?"

"Running off with one woman, I can understand. But I assure you four would never pass in South Kensington."

"The whole picture is completely and totally false," Miles declared. "It was all cooked up, my love, honestly. All for the —well, for the divorce."

"So, Miles, you really intend to force me into divorcing you?"

"No, no, no!" exclaimed Miles. "Not for a moment, really. Nothing was further from my thoughts."

Connie raised her eyebrows. "Then what are you up to, for heaven's sake? Running a fresh-air home for the ladies of London?"

"I told you, it's entirely a put-up job. It was Gaston who made me do all this."

"So." Connie eyed me.

"Here, I say—" I protested.

"I begin to see," added Connie.

"Look here, Connie, it's nothing whatever to do with me—"

"Did you or did you not organize this present gathering?" Connie demanded.

"Well . . . yes, of course, I organized it," I admitted shortly. "You don't suppose Miles could have risen to it, do you?"

"Oh," said Connie quietly.

"I shall positively expire if I don't have a cigarette this very minute," Dolores informed everyone.

"Perhaps we'd better be going, dear," murmured Gertie.

"Yes, it's been lovely," agreed Cissy.

The dog finished eating Miles's sponge bag and, finding itself at a loose end, sat under the washbasin and barked.

"I see," Connie went on. "You, Gaston, worked your wicked wiles to estrange us, so that you could slip round behind your own cousin's back and thrust your bestial intentions on me."

"What's all this?" demanded Miles, advancing on me a bit.

"I like that!" I now felt thoroughly narked. "I've never thrust anything on Connie in my life, except those cheap olives you provide at those rotten parties of yours."

"Pustule," muttered Miles, who seemed to have made a complete recovery from his attack of vertigo. "Pathogenic organism."

"Coo," said Gertie.

"If I can't have a cigarette, I must have a drink," remarked Dolores. "Do you suppose if I ring the bell it will get up the old man from the hall?"

"Miles, you fool!" I brought down my fist on the commode. "Surely you can't really believe I'm a snake wriggling in your front lawn? Dash it, I'm your cousin! I'd never dream of misbehaving myself in the slightest with Connie."

"He tried the other week," said Connie evenly. "Twice."

"Leprous bacterium," growled Miles, approaching closer.

"But can't you understand? I agreed to help Connie with the divorce only for old times' sake—"

"Old times *what*, you moral streptococcus?" muttered Miles.

"Well . . . damnation, I mean to say, Connie and I were mildly chummy before you slid her up to the altar . . ."

"Gaston, you putrefying abscess! You never told me this."

"*Mildly* chummy," I repeated. "I merely took her up the river when you were on duty at St. Swithin's. I thought you knew. And anyway, what the hell's the odds at this stage?"

"It was at this very hotel," chipped in Connie, "that Gaston and I stayed the weekend he drove me down to Whortleton."

"You toxin," cried Miles, and caught me no end of a sock in the epigastric region.

The Jellybone Sisters gave a scream, the dog started barking again, and someone in the next room began hammering on the wall.

"What sort of a hotel is this?" demanded Dolores. "Nobody answers the bells."

"Miles!" exclaimed Connie, as I bent, puffing, over the commode. "How wonderful you are."

"As much as I decry the use of brute force, my love, I would never hesitate to use it to expunge any smear on the name of my dear wife."

"Oh, Miles! Just look at Gaston—the way he's gasping. How strong you must be!"

"Although I naturally pride myself on my intellectual attainments—even more perhaps than on my strength of character—I assure you that self-appreciation of my physical prowess is curbed only by my natural modesty."

"Darling Miles," breathed Connie, collapsing on him.

"Come, beloved. Now let us make our way back to our little home."

"Here, I say," I protested, rubbing my middle. "You two can't just clear off and leave me alone with the ruddy harem."

"Why not, pray?" glared Miles, shoveling the bits of sponge bag into his case. "You got yourself into the mess. You can't expect me to get you out again."

"I am sure," added Connie, "that a man of Gaston's type will not be slow to take the utmost advantage of his present company."

"I'm about sick and tired of the way you're carrying on toward me, Connie," I exploded, "just because you've decided you want to saddle old Miles again. It was a different story that evening you came round to my flat with the woolly slippers. You were all over me, to get me in the frame of mind to fix up this ghastly business."

"How dare you talk to my wife like that," rasped Miles, advancing again. "I intend to deal you further trauma in the abdomen."

"Don't waste your strength, my precious," said Connie. "The creature isn't worth it."

"We really must be going, and that's a fact," announced Gertie.

"Doesn't anyone answer the damned bells in this place?" complained Dolores.

"I will treat you with the contempt you deserve." Miles picked up his suitcase. "Please pack up my things in your flat and have them sent round by messenger. How fortunate, my love," he continued to Connie, "that you found your way here before Gaston dragged me to even murkier depths."

"Hey! How the devil did Connie know where you were anyway?"

"Naturally, I left my address." Miles scowled from the door. "I am still expecting any moment a summons from Mr. Odysseus."

"Oh, the summons," said Connie. "It's arrived."

"Excellent," said Miles.

Connie gave a little laugh. "Yes, for assault. He was the one you hit in the night club."

"Oh," said Miles.

"He called to see you that day, and I felt the least I could do was agree to show him the sights."

"Oh," said Miles.

"But I don't think he's going to proceed with the case, because he's gone back to Greece. Taking his moneybags with him, I'm afraid."

"Oh," said Miles.

"Which jolly well serves you right," I shouted.

He slammed the door.

Chapter Twenty

~

There was a silence. I gave my middle another rub and rapidly tried to sort things out. I may have had all manner of internal bruising in the abdomen, I reflected, but at least I had the consolation of Miles coming out of the affair worse than me. The Odysseus millions certainly wouldn't oil his way toward the House of Lords, after a few years sweating it out among the delinquents. And now Miles was out of the room the Whortleton situation began to clear a little. All I had to do was disperse the troops, pass a day recovering in the sea breezes, then meet Dame Hilda and Anemone off the London train on Monday afternoon as arranged, with some story about Miles and his missus having leapt at the chance of a spare bed by the briny. Meanwhile, I had to get some sleep.

"Right ho, ladies, thank you very much," I announced. "I think it's time the party broke up. And so does that chap in the next room, by the way he's hammering on the wall."

"It's been delightful," said Gertie.

"Yes, ever so," agreed Cissy.

"We hardly ever go out these days at all," added Joan.

"Glad you've enjoyed it. If you will now allow me to escort you downstairs—"

"There's just one thing," said Gertie.

"Yes, there is, isn't there?" Cissy nodded.

"Just a very little thing," concurred Joan.

"What little thing?" I asked, rather shortly.

"Our cash," said Gertie.

"The lolly," pointed out Cissy.

"Yes, the crinkly," observed Joan.

"Our hundred quid."

"A promise is a promise."

"Your friend never gave us the check."

"You might give me mine while you're at it, darling," interrupted Dolores, still pressing the bell.

"Don't worry about the check, girls," I said lightly. "My friend may be a worm, but I guarantee he'll be perfectly honorable and send you the money as soon as he remembers in the morning. Otherwise, of course, he'd be scared stiff of you blackmailing him."

"I'd rather have it now, please," said Gertie.

"On the nail."

"Fair's fair."

"It's useless asking me," I told the three Jellybones. "Because I haven't got a hundred quid."

"We're not leaving till we've been paid," insisted Gertie. "And believe me, we've had plenty of experience getting our proper rights from nasty managements before now."

"Remember what we did at Blackpool?" asked Cissy.

"When they had to call the police," Joan reminded her.

"If no one answers this bell soon I'm going to scream," said Dolores.

"For lord's sake be reasonable!" I remonstrated. "I promise you'll all be paid within the next twenty-four hours. If you like, I'll actually ring up the blasted chap and remind him. Though if you would care to blackmail him, anyway," I added, "it's perfectly all right with me."

"No cash, no go," said the Jellybone Sisters at once.

"If you're being sticky with the money, darling," added

Dolores, "I'd like to remind you I've some very strong-minded gentlemen friends in town."

"Now look here, I've had more than enough pushing about for one evening," I announced, losing patience with the blasted gaggle. "If you ladies want to stay in Whortleton until doomsday you're welcome to the room. Personally I'm pushing off to doss down under the pier. Good night!"

As I grabbed my raincoat there was a knock on the door.

The porter appeared.

"Excuse me bothering you again, sir. But I have a gentleman here who seems anxious to see you. Name of Sir Lancelot Spratt."

"Sir Lancelot—?"

"All right, porter, I'll let myself in if the boy's not asleep," came the familiar voice from outside. "Ah, Grimsdyke, there you are—what the devil's going on here? What are all these people doing? Take that damned dog away," he added, coming into the bedroom with Dame Hilda and Anemone.

"Who," demanded Dame Hilda generally, "are you?"

"Mrs. Grimsdyke," said all my four guests.

"I can explain everything," I started.

"Please don't."

"Look here, Grimsdyke, if I had known you were this type of feller I certainly wouldn't have taken you to New York last month."

"New York? I thought you were in Cheltenham."

"Well—er, not quite Cheltenham, actually."

Dame Hilda turned to Anemone. "Please give it to me, my child."

"Give you what, Mummy?"

"The ring, naturally. Sir Lancelot, perhaps you would drive us to some other accommodation? As for you, Dr. Grimsdyke, when I imagined you had merely forgotten to cancel these rooms I was blissfully unaware of the depravity concealed below your deceptively witless exterior. Come, Anemone."

"I should like to see you, Grimsdyke, in the morning," ended Sir Lancelot. "You will meet me at nine by the bandstand."

They left.

"Will that be all, sir?" asked the porter.

"I sincerely hope so," I told him.

He sighed. "Dear me, sir. We have a lot to learn I fear, sir."

"How right you are," I agreed.

I managed to get rid of the Jellybones in the end by giving them a check for fifty quid on account. Dolores spent the night in number ten, and I slept in Miles's room, with the dog. And in the morning the ruddy kippers were cold anyway.

Chapter Twenty-One

~

I was brokenhearted, of course. The evening had bulldozed my life to ruins. Miles and Connie regarded me no longer as their private marriage counselor, but as a refugee from the Reptile House gone to earth in the family bosom. And instead of being engaged to the nicest girl in the world I had only an ache in my soul and a ring in my pocket, which I bet I wouldn't get more than fifty per cent back on, either.

Equally galling, I felt, as I made my way back to London alone that Sunday morning, was nobody believing my innocence. I was as shining white as if recently rubbed down by one of those ruddy detergents that kept appearing in the middle of my television program. And the whole world was insisting on treating me like Jack the Ripper's little brother.

"I must say, Grimsdyke, your stature has grown considerably in my estimation," Sir Lancelot had started genially at the bandstand. "To take one girl to the seaside under the nose of one's prospective mother-in-law is quite an achievement. But four! My dear feller, Don Juan himself would have thrown in the sponge. And that's not even taking account of the dog."

"I assure you, sir," I insisted hastily, "there is a perfectly proper explanation."

"It is quite unnecessary to try it on me. I am no schoolboy, Grimsdyke. I understand these things. It is, incidentally," he added, "equally unnecessary for you to try it on Dame Hilda. She simply wouldn't listen."

"I rather felt that would be the case, sir," I said dully.

"All bad luck on you, of course," Sir Lancelot continued cheerfully, as we strolled in the early breezes along the prom.

"I still can't understand," I confessed, feeling like the remains of the Light Brigade at Balaklava, "exactly why you three turned up here at all."

"I rather fear you must lay the blame for that on my wife."

"On Lady Spratt, sir?"

"Yes. When Dame Hilda's party of delinquent teen-agers followed us down from London, she promptly sent their motorbus back again. It was very strange," remarked Sir Lancelot, exchanging a glance with the stuffed shark outside the aquarium. "I had always believed my wife and Dame Hilda to be such firm friends. But my wife was behaving oddly the entire two days before the girls joined us. I must confess she made something of a scene just because Dame Hilda kept inviting me to tell my favorite fishing stories and show her how delightful the rose garden looked in the moonlight. I fancy the stay in Majorca did my wife no good. As the atmosphere became somewhat strained and I had business in London anyway, I agreed, after telephoning you vainly, to drive Dame Hilda down here. With her daughter—who, let me tell you, my boy, is not one quarter the woman that her mother is."

"Quite, sir."

Sir Lancelot paused to set his watch by the floral clock. "I must confess that I should have preferred to pass the night as arranged in the room reserved for yourself, instead of a commercial hotel with beds I intend to report to the British Travel Association and sanitation I intend to report to the Medical Officer of Health. But doubtless you put the accommodation to better use."

"Really, sir, I swear there was nothing—"

"You are returning to London by rail? I fear I can hardly offer you a lift. My car is not nearly large enough for all your wives and their luggage."

There was one compensation, I reflected, as I made my way from Victoria Station toward my horses' larder. At least I'd got rid of Miles, just as it was coming up for his turn on the divan again, too. I had a couple of hours' hard work ahead packing up the chap's junk, I calculated as I mounted the narrow stairs and felt for the key, then for the first time in weeks I should be able to lie back and spread myself and take as long as I liked in the bath.

I opened the front door. Lying on the divan in his shirt sleeves with a box of my special Christmas cigars was Squiffy.

"How the devil did you get in?" I demanded crossly from the threshold.

"Grim, my dear chap!" Squiffy leapt up, spilling the cigars. "Thank heavens you've arrived! Through the window, of course," he added.

"Through the window? And why, pray?" I asked, as icily as a morning dip at Whortleton.

"But the front door was locked," he explained.

I sat on the divan.

"Grim, I simply had to see you," Squiffy went on, taking off his glasses and scratching his head with them. "I got your address from Lucy. Though she hasn't the first idea I'm round here. Or about the beastly jam I'm in. But, honestly, you're the only chap in the world who can possibly help me. I'm being persecuted by the Kremlin."

Paranoia, of course, I diagnosed. Persecution mania. A lot of it about. I'd always thought Squiffy was mad, since he'd painted pink the pet hedgehog he kept in the dorm and wrote poetry to it. I decided I'd better quietly humor the poor chap and hope he wouldn't go berserk, not that there was much room in my flat for anyone to go berserk decently anyway.

"Grim, I desperately need advice."

"You desperately need a drink first, if you ask me," I told him, making for the kitchen sink.

"My old man will kill me."

"You mean, he's turned up and discovered that instead of telling the government where to put its atoms you're telling grubby little boys that sugar mixed with sodium chlorate makes a hell of a bang?"

"No, I'm on holiday at the moment." Squiffy sat trying to detach his left hand at the radiocarpal joint. "And Father's been held up in Karachi for another month, which is just as well, as they've sent in the bill for the lab I burnt down in Mireborough. I suppose you couldn't lend me five hundred quid, could you?"

"There, there," I said, offering a sympathetic glass and shifting a few of my breakables out of his reach. The chap was clearly having delusions as well. "Why can't you just ring up the bank and ask them to send a boy round with it?"

"My old man would kill me in a rather more painful way, that's all. You know his odd ideas of keeping me and the millions separated? I had to borrow five hundred for day-to-day expenses from the head beak at the school—a mean blighter, counts the nibs and chalk—on the strength of Father's name. Though mind you," Squiffy added, the family financial acumen showing through, "if you could raise only fifty quid and we put it on a real cert at ten to one, it would do just as well, wouldn't it?"

"Yes, but what's all this got to do with you being persecuted by chaps with beards and snow on their boots?"

Squiffy paused. "Do you suppose that actor chap, Basil Beauchamp, when he's finished being Hamlet for the evening goes home and moons about, muttering 'Alas! poor Yorick,' and so on?"

"No, he generally goes out and has no end of a time of it with your sister."

"That's the point. Once he's given the customers their money's worth of Hamlet he goes on being Basil Beauchamp again—not that I've much to say in favor of that." Squiffy took a gulp from his glass. "My trouble, Grim, is being carried away by my part. It was fair enough covering up that little trouble at Mireborough by spreading the rumor I'm a top scientist round the family. But . . . well, when you go to a party and some girl asks you what you do in life, you can't just explain your days are dedicated to teaching a bunch of kids how the hall barometer works. You say you're a scientist, and her eyes light up and she says, How fascinating, I suppose you make hydrogen bombs and space ships, and you say, Naturally, and in no time at all you're out in the garden pointing out the galaxies."

I remembered that Squiffy was quite a one for the girls, and in the old days at Whortleton had a terrific pash on some little blonde number with a plastic windmill.

"I was holding forth like this at an odd sort of party out in Notting Hill to a girl called Noreen—very decent type, works one of those wonderful machines in an espresso bar, all steam, I wish I could. Then this little fellow Yarmouth oiled up," Squiffy explained. "A funny bird, largely moustache and glasses. But he's an absolutely top-of-the-bill secret agent."

"Look here, Squiffy, you can't really expect me to believe—"

"Damn it, Grim, you're always reading about them in the papers. Ordinary-looking fellows who walk into the Admiralty saying they've come to clean the windows and stuff all the plans up their jumpers. I was expanding a bit about life at Woomera—" Squiffy suddenly scratched his head. "Where is Woomera, by the way? I suppose I'd had a few noggins, because I was holding forth on the international situation as well when Yarmouth went a bit shifty and asked if I'd like to meet his comrades. I thought he meant for a game of darts or something, so I said, Yes, and he said, Go to the British Museum next Sunday with a copy of the Telephone Directory E to K and a string bag containing three oranges—or it may have been lemons, I forget, or even grapefruit—and approach the chap with the Telephone Directory L to R and a string of onions, and say that your grandmother has broken her spectacles. He'd reply that homemade brawn was very nourishing, and we'd be in business."

"My dear Squiffy," I explained. "This is only some fellow-maniac—"

"What do you mean, 'fellow'?" Squiffy looked offended. "All this started before Lucy got back from New York. Naturally, I never turned up that Sunday, and a weekend or so later Yarmouth phoned me. Got my number from Noreen, you see. He seemed pretty narked, too. Beastly place for anyone to wait about, the British Museum, I suppose. He still rings up wanting me to meet his chum with the onions—what was that?"

It was a knock at the door. Squiffy plunged behind the divan.

"My dear old lad, don't panic! It isn't the bloke from Moscow, it's only the neighbors come to scrounge some cigarettes. Why, hello." I smiled, opening the door. "Quite a surprise."

"Hello, Gaston." Lucy smiled back from the mat. "I've come to find my brother."

"Your brother?"

"Yes, he's the man with his foot sticking up behind your divan."

"How on earth did you know I was here?" demanded Squiffy crossly, restoring himself among those present.

"My dear, it was as obvious as Nelson in Trafalgar Square from the way you wanted the address."

"I just called to have a chat with Gaston. About my work, you know. In the laboratory."

"Exactly. And I have just called to say your laboratory has

rung urgently to complain that you've left with the keys of the sweet shop."

"Ah, yes," explained Squiffy. " 'Sweet Shop.' Code name for our latest secret bomb. Very destructive."

"I couldn't find the keys in your room," Lucy went on levelly. "Only an exercise book containing some formulas corrected by you in red ink—extremely untidily, if I may say so— with a remarkably lifelike pencil sketch of yourself on the back page over the caption 'Stinkers is a Fool.' May I come in?"

"Yes, of course."

"You are heartless, Gaston," Lucy added sweetly to me. "Not so much as phoning to say what happened to that lovely divorce."

"I just thought you'd be terribly occupied with charity matinees and Basil Beauchamp, and so on."

"Basil's away at the moment. He's having quite a time, going round judging seaside beauty contests looking for his musical Saint Joan."

I remembered noticing through the haze that Basil was visiting the Whortleton Holiday Camp to judge the national finals the following Saturday.

"Lucy, I can explain everything," burst out Squiffy, who had been making asphyxiated noises on the divan.

"Please do."

"You see, Lucy—" He scratched his head. "Oh, hell! You tell her, Grim."

I briefly described her brother's standing in scientific and espionage circles.

"George," Lucy summed up. "You're a fool."

"That's all very well, but I can't even ask for police protection, or whatever it is. Then the cats would be out of the bag and being sick all over the carpet by the time the old man got home."

"I can assure you this Yarmouth is simply pulling your leg," said Lucy calmly.

I must say, I admired the cool way she took charge of the proceedings. I remembered Lucy had a great knack for handling awkward situations, even in those days at Whortleton when Squiffy somehow managed to sit on himself while putting up a deck chair.

"You don't know how nasty he can seem on the phone, particularly rather early in the morning," grumbled Squiffy. "I've never known anyone who could give the words 'British Museum' such a sinister ring."

"It so happens that all the British Museum business is exactly the same as an episode that Basil did on television weeks ago."

"Really?" Squiffy brightened up. "Of course I always watch the puppets on the other channel."

"Even to the telephone directories and the oranges."

"Then it sounds as if the chap really is a spoof?"

"Making two of you," I remarked.

"George," said Lucy firmly. "You need a rest."

"You're jolly well not getting rid of me to our country place. You know the butler down there gets his wages put up every time he reports to the old man something nasty I've done."

"You could go abroad."

"My passport has been in the vaults since the business of that girl on the Costa Brava. Anyway I can't go away," Squiffy pointed out. "Now Basil's hareing round the coast, I'm supposed to be taking you to Lord's and Glyndebourne this week."

Lucy smiled. "I'm sure Gaston would take me instead—if you've no other commitments."

"Who me?" That sunset broke out again inside. "Yes, of course, Lucy. I've got no other commitments at all. None whatever. I say, let's have a lunch-time drink," I suggested eagerly. I glanced round. "Except that George seems to have killed the bottle."

"I'll get another from the pub on the corner." Squiffy leapt up. "After the terrific relief about Yarmouth it's absolutely the least I can do."

"Gaston, you certainly lack the woman's touch," remarked Lucy, looking round as Squiffy disappeared.

"Bit untidy, I admit. Had a relative to stay."

"I insist you let me smooth the surface, anyway." She pushed up her sleeves. "What on earth do you do with this ghastly thing in a bottle?"

"That's my relative's. It came out of a High Court judge."

"Ugh," said Lucy and started to sort out the crockery.

I could never have entertained Lucy alone in my flat while still engaged to the nicest girl in the world, of course. But now, I reflected, as I fingered the obsolete ring in my pocket, I could entertain all the women in London I liked to, though even a few of them would have made quite a crowd.

"Lucy," I mentioned, as she started wielding the broom with advanced alopecia. "I thought you were booked for that part of Basil's singing saint?"

She gave a little pout, which brought the sunset back to the pylorus.

"Oh, he seemed to think my voice hadn't enough appeal and my legs had too much or something. You know, Gaston—Basil's a dear, and knows absolutely everyone on the stage—but I sometimes wonder if he might be more interested in my father's finances than in me."

"Oh, come!" I was quite horrified. "Dear old Basil's one of the best. I've been chummy with him for years."

"Yes, I suppose it's only my female intuition, and nothing's quite so unreliable as that."

"Admittedly, of course, he's rather vain. But then all actors are."

"Um, yes," said Lucy, raking a harvest of cigarette packets from under the divan.

"I'd be quite unbearably vain myself if I had his looks. And with all the girls falling for me."

"All the girls?"

I laughed. "An occupational hazard with actors, you know. Sometimes you can hardly hear his lines in the stalls for the snapping of broken hearts."

"Um, yes," said Lucy again.

"And of course, he *does* wear scent."

"Scent? But he told me it was some lotion the doctor advised for his skin."

I laughed again.

"Basil has very charming manners," insisted Lucy, picking up three or four old socks.

"Yes, that's what the landlady's daughter used to say in our digs. Poor girl! I wonder how it all turned out after she'd had her . . . her holiday."

"Gaston!" Lucy suddenly threw down the broom. "Basil expects me to marry him."

"Congratulations. Very decent husband, I'm sure. Good provider, always cheerful about the house, careful dresser, tells a good anecdote—"

Lucy stamped her foot. "Gaston, can't you turn off your insane drivel for one moment? Don't you see I'm serious?"

"Here, I say, Lucy, I didn't realize—"

"Oh, Gaston! I did promise him, and I don't really want to now at all," cried Lucy.

And there she was, weeping on my shoulder, just like Connie, but a jolly sight nicer.

"There, there," I said, hoping my hanky wasn't too mucky after the rough night at Whortleton.

"Dear Gaston," sobbed Lucy. "You're—you're such a psychological aspirin."

"Always ready to treat a case of acute distress in the damsel, I assure you."

Lucy swallowed. "I've thought about you so much, Gaston dear."

"Go on?" was all I could manage, what with the sunset spreading up the esophagus and down into the duodenum.

"I've thought about those lovely days we had together as kids in Whortleton. And how you were so frightfully brave about taking that bee off my neck."

"Ah, that bee."

"The other day Basil wouldn't even dare kill a mosquito on my collar."

"I mightn't be much cop at mosquitoes myself," I admitted. "I'm strictly a bee man."

"Gaston—do you remember when you kissed me?"

"Behind the whelks, wasn't it?"

"No. By the outfall."

"Yes, you were wearing your little one-piece."

"I've never forgotten it."

"As a matter of fact, Lucy," I told her truthfully, "neither have I."

"Kiss me again, Gaston," Lucy started to say.

But I already had.

"What on earth's going on in here?" shouted Squiffy through the letter box. "I've been knocking for simply hours. Have you lost all interest in drink, or something?"

"And now—" Lucy smiled, taking my hand as I opened the door—"Gaston's coming home with us for lunch."

Chapter Twenty-Two

The next morning I was woken by a terrific knocking on my front door.

I sat up on the divan, feeling confused. I'd just experienced the most wonderful day in my life. I'd lunched in Lucy's flat, then we'd gone for a walk in the park, where somehow we'd lost Squiffy. There admittedly wasn't much to do for the rest of Sunday because of Miles and his moral chums, but I managed to find a restaurant open to buy Lucy dinner, and afterwards she said she'd love to drink beer in a little pub I remembered snuggling among the warehouses on Bankside. Then we walked hand in hand along the Embankment, baring the old soul a bit and looking at the lights sparking on the bridges, and feeling that Nature was after all creeping up on the late James Whistler. Before I'd even looked at my watch it was already long past midnight.

I now looked at my watch again, and found it was already long past ten. I supposed I'd been pretty tired, not having much sleep the night before on emotional tenterhooks down at Whortleton, not to mention a mattress apparently stuffed with dried seaweed.

"All right, all right," I shouted, as the terrific knocking was repeated. "Don't bash the ruddy thing off its hinges."

I pulled on a dressing gown, wondering who the devil it was. Miles again, to say he'd had a second bust-up with Connie and

asking me kindly to fix another divorce? Or it might have been
Squiffy, after wandering all night in the park. Or perhaps just
Mr. Hildenborough come for the empties.

"Half a jiffy, blast it!" I called to another burst of terrific
knocking. "Damn it, what have you got out there? Twelve
halberdiers and a battering-ram?"

I threw open the door. On the mat stood Dame Hilda and
Anemone.

"You poor, poor boy," cried Dame Hilda.

She enfolded me to her bosom, which was like being
trapped in a padded cell.

"You poor, poor, dear boy."

"Er—good morning, Dame Hilda. Lovely day, isn't it?"

"You poor dear misunderstood thing!"

"Good morning, Anemone." We Grimsdykes remember our
manners, whatever the hour. "Would you care to step inside? A
cup of coffee? I must apologize for the stubble and slippers,
but I forgot to wind my alarm clock. Remarkable how one goes
on sleeping—"

"How can you ever forgive me?" exploded Dame Hilda.

"Nothing to forgive, I'm sure," I returned politely, reaching
for the coffeepot.

"I mean, about Saturday night down at Whortleton."

I gave a little laugh. "Oh, that? Yes, rather a ruined evening
all round, wasn't it?"

Dame Hilda gazed at me. "Gaston, how I admire the brave
gaiety with which you hide from the hard world your inner
suffering."

"Oh, I don't know—"

"Just like Sir Philip Sidney."

"It's a gay sort of morning, with the sun and the birds and all
that," I pointed out.

"Then I shall complete your enjoyment of it. I have heard
all."

"Oh, have you, Dame Hilda? A piece of toast, perhaps?"

"Sir Lancelot—such a wonderful man in so many respects—seemed to have had his suspicions of that cousin of yours, Miles. He went straight to his house on arriving in London, and learned the whole story. When Sir Lancelot telephoned me last night I saw how unjust and unkind I had been. You are unblemished with a speck of blame."

"Very decent of you, Dame Hilda. Marmalade?"

"The whole fantastic affair was merely an emotional storm on the part of Miles's wife. Quite reasonable in her condition. Before next spring, young Bartholomew will have a playmate."

"Good lord, so that's the diagnosis, is it? No wonder she was so keen on the ruddy coconuts."

"As far as you are concerned, Gaston—" Dame Hilda smiled —"all is as it ever was."

"That's fine," I agreed. "I must say, I don't much like going about under a cloud. Particularly as I never seem to have my brolly when they start raining on me."

"Mummy means about us," chipped in Anemone, for the first time. "You and me. Everything's all right again."

"Ah, yes," I said. "You and me."

It was an odd thing, but somehow I'd rather got to regarding Anemone as all cut and dried.

"Gaston, my dear child," went on Dame Hilda, getting me in the padded cell again. "Where's the ring?"

I fished the thing out of my tobacco jar.

"Slip it straight back on Anemone's finger. That's right. How wonderful to see you two young people so happy again!"

"We certainly are. Aren't we, Nenny?" I asked.

"We must decide the happy day at once," declared her mother.

"I think I hear the coffee boiling—"

"Now you are reunited in joy, I would suggest Saturday in a week. What on earth's the matter, Gaston?"

"Nothing, Dame Hilda. Nothing at all. It's just that Saturday in a week might be a bit of a rush."

"A rush? But you have," she indicated, with a touch of the old fire, "already had the better part of two years to think about it."

"Yes, I suppose I have."

"Saturday in a week would be extremely convenient. Naturally, I canceled the rooms at the Surfview, so Anemone and I have our two weeks holiday completely free to make all the preparations in Yorkshire."

"Sure you wouldn't like a bite of toast? Or I could do you an egg, if you'd care."

"No thank you, Gaston. A fortnight's hard work, with my powers of administration, will have everything absolutely shipshape. A pity my dear husband persists on those long expeditions to South America, but I fancy that I can persuade Sir Lancelot to give Anemone away. Who have you in mind for your best man?"

I felt a bit blank. "There's a friend of mine, an atomic scientist. He's on holiday at the moment, so I suppose he could make it."

"Your end is settled then."

"I suppose it is."

"Anemone and I shall get on with the job by taking the morning train from King's Cross tomorrow. I shall order the cake from Fortnum's this afternoon."

"Mummy," chipped in Anemone again. "What about the girls?"

"Thank you, my child. I was quite forgetting. Owing to Lady Spratt's remarkable behavior, my party of maladjusted teen-agers was bitterly disappointed over their holiday in Wales. Before Sir Lancelot telephoned yesterday, I had arranged for them to spend a week at the Whortleton holiday camp instead. As Anemone and I must go north to prepare the wedding, perhaps you—and your best man, if he has no commitments— would like to occupy the chalet we booked for ourselves? I would feel happier if there was someone like you, Gaston, a qualified doctor, to keep an eye on them. Besides, I'm sure a few days at the seaside before you get married will do you the world of good."

"I did have one or two odd jobs—"

"I won't take no for an answer, you know." She smiled. "Besides, it will keep you out of mischief—give you something to do—while awaiting the happy day to dawn."

"Oh, very well, Dame Hilda," I agreed.

"You must call me Mother. Come, Anemone. We have much work to do. Be at the coach station tomorrow at nine, Gaston, to collect the girls. I hand-picked them myself, and you will find them perfectly well behaved."

They left. I sat on the divan. The sun was still shining, the birds were still singing, the milkman was cheerfully clinking and whistling down in the mews, and the geraniums in the window box were nodding a genial good morning to the cats. But somehow summer seemed to have gone into monochrome. I gave another one of those sighs. What, I asked myself, was I worrying about? After all, I was now quite shortly and quite definitely to be joined in matrimony with absolutely the nicest girl in the world.

Chapter Twenty-Three

~

"I say, Grim." Squiffy scratched his head with his glasses. "What did that fat old woman mean when she said I was your best man?"

"She meant you were the best man I could find for the job."

"Oh, I see. Though it's not much in my line, this sort of thing, really."

"As a practising chemistry master, you ought to have the right touch."

"I'll be glad to get out of town, though, once we're started." Squiffy twisted his legs on the back seat of the bus until they looked as if they'd need surgery to untangle them again. "Things hang rather heavy at this time of the year. Then there's always the chance of that chap Yarmouth showing up. Besides, I've wanted to go to a holiday camp for years. They look quite a treat in the commercials on the telly."

I gave a grunt.

"I say, Grim, what's up with you today? You look as if maggots were eating into your soul."

"Bit preoccupied, that's all. Sudden welfare job like this. We doctors have to take our responsibilities seriously."

"I dunno, it's lovely weather and everyone seems to be moping about. I left Lucy with a face like a wet Sunday in Scotland."

"Oh, yes?" I said, brightening up a little.

"She seemed pretty disappointed you were suddenly called away. I think she was looking forward to you taking her to Lord's and Glyndebourne."

"Of course, she's fond of cricket and opera."

"No, she isn't very much, of either."

"Hold on," I told him. "We're off."

Our private bus slid out of Victoria coach station into the sunshine, bearing our dozen girls toward the morally therapeutic breezes of Whortleton.

"I know with these hand-picked girls it is quite unnecessary to warn you, Gaston," Dame Hilda had said, before hurrying away with Anemone to catch their train. "But we do have certain little rules I'd like you to observe. Bed by nine, a cold wash every morning, and no smokes, drinks, or of course sex. Here is a pound for you to buy them some sweeties if they're very good girls indeed."

"Good-bye, Ma'am, and God bless you," cried all the girls at once.

"Have a lovely holiday," Dame Hilda called back. "Don't forget to write."

I kissed Anemone good-bye while Squiffy was looking for his luggage, which he'd lost already. I somehow hadn't introduced my fiancée to him. Come to think of it, Anemone was the sort of girl who nobody somehow introduced to anyone. I climbed aboard, relieved to see the girls looking so demure in their white frocks and straight hair. They seemed between about twelve and sixteen, rather given to acne and strabismus, but otherwise presenting the healthy carbolic appearance of any outing from any sort of institution.

"Odd to be going down to Whortleton again," remarked Squiffy, as our driver turned toward South London. "I've been thinking of the old place a good deal since we met up. And so has Lucy. Last night she even dug out an old photograph of the three of us with our buckets and spades and stuck it up on her dressing table."

"Oh, yes?" I said again.

Squiffy paused, trying to disarticulate his left metacarpo-phalangeal joints.

"Grim," he exclaimed, "is there anything on between you and Lucy?"

"On? Nothing whatsoever."

"I mean, she's shifted the picture of Basil as Romeo into the bathroom. Though mind you," he reflected, "she's still got him as Mark Anthony, King Lear, and Othello. No, come to think of it, she shoved the Othello one away in a drawer this morning."

"Lucy is merely one of my dear old chums. Just like you."

I sat back in my seat. I was determined to do absolutely the right thing by my fiancée, who was the nicest female of the species. Though I couldn't help feeling slightly like the fatted calf when it heard the Prodigal Son's footsteps crunching up the drive.

I gave a sniff.

"I say, Squiffy, do you suppose the bus is on fire?"

He sniffed, too. "Yes, there is a bit of a pong, certainly."

"Look there's some smoke coming from up front," I exclaimed, hurrying down the aisle with the idea of saving the little victims from the blaze.

In the front seat were two twelve-year-olds, puffing away at a couple of home-rolled.

"Er—little girl—" I began to the one with the acne.

"Aw, go and get yourself stuffed with gooseberries."

"Here, I say!" I felt a bit hot in the cervical region. "You two put those fags out immediately."

The one with the squint chipped in with a few of the words they put in asterisks in the evening papers.

"I told you to put that ruddy fag out," I repeated firmly.

This brought uproar from the bus, the sort of thing described in the Parliamentary reports as "Shouts of Oh! and Resign" and also a few more asterisks from the squint.

"Oh, all right, Lady Chatterley," I told her. "Smoke as much as you ruddy well like, and to hell with your bronchial epithelium."

I stalked back to my seat, feeling nettled.

"Hey, lover man," invited one of the older girls who had done such a nice curtsy for Dame Hilda. "Want a drag?"

"Thanks." I took a couple of cigarettes from her packet. "And I'll have one for my friend, too."

Squiffy and I lit up, feeling I'd put the little blighter in her place with a show of democratic mateyness, while the girls quieted down a bit, possibly because we were passing Wandsworth Jail, and quite a few were peering excitedly for their dads.

"Here, I say," complained Squiffy. "What sort of a brand of cigarette is this?"

"I suppose she rolls them herself," I suggested, inspecting the thing. "It seems the fashion."

I took a few more puffs.

"I say, Squiffy—" I gave a bit of a laugh. "This little outing isn't going to be too bad after all."

Squiffy gave a bit of a laugh too. "That's better, Grim! You're starting to cheer up."

"Oh, life isn't such a rotten institution, when you come to think of it."

I flicked off my ash gaily.

"It's odd—" Squiffy grinned—"but I was just thinking myself the world's a pretty larky place, by and large."

"And these kids—not a bad bunch at heart."

"Nothing wrong with the coming generation, believe me."

I laughed again. "I do believe the little rascals have got a gin bottle down there."

"I say! What fun they're having."

"Does your heart good to see them."

"Girls will be girls."

We both thought this terribly funny.

"I wonder," I went on, wiping the tears away, "if you've heard the frightfully amusing story of the bishop and the parrot?"

"I can hardly wait," cried Squiffy, slapping his thighs.

"I'll tell you." I giggled. "If we've got a moment before we arrive at Whortleton."

Squiffy roared with laughter. "But we haven't left London yet, you old chump!"

"I say, haven't we?" I roared back. "But we left London at lunch time."

"Lunch time? I'm sure we didn't. We left London last night."

"Perhaps we did." I thought again. "No, we've got it wrong, Squiffy. We left London tomorrow morning."

I suddenly noticed Anemone coming up the aisle between the seats, just finishing the Dance of the Seven Veils.

"I say!" I exclaimed, sitting back to enjoy the finale. "You don't get this sort of thing on London Transport—" I grabbed Squiffy's arm. "That cigarette—put the ruddy thing out at once."

"Eh? Come off it, Grim. I'm rather enjoying the smoke. Jolly good mind to change my brand."

"Put it out, man!"

I was a bit fuddled, but I managed to sort out the diagnosis. Distortion of sense of time and space, I seemed to remember from the pharmacology books, with fatuous cheerfulness and striking visions of a markedly erotic nature. The symptoms of intoxication by cannabis indica, also known as marijuana, bhang, dagga, hashish, or Indian hemp.

"Where's the girl with those cigarettes?" I demanded. "Here, you—you little horror. Do you realize you're smoking reefers?"

She gave me a look. "Lover boy, ain't you learnt nuffink? You don't get no kicks out of a packet of Woods when yer bin on the drag as long as yours truly."

"Hand over that packet at once. Do you hear me? Don't you realize it's a dangerous drug?"

"Garn. Cost me a quid, these did. Buy your own, you old skinflint."

This argument being taken up by the rest of the meeting, there wasn't much for it except retreat. On the back seat I found Squiffy struggling with a girl on his knee who was trying to bite his ear.

"Grim! For lord's sake get this sex kitten out of my hair," he cried pitifully.

"Stop that at once," I commanded.

She gave me a look of contempt. "Be yer age, Mister, be yer age."

Luckily, at that point the Lady Chatterley girl distracted everybody by starting a singsong.

Mind you, I used to be pretty useful at the old hospital singing, particularly late at night when all the girls had disappeared and the chaps could let themselves go with some of the sporty old favorites. But the ripe clinical songs round the beer barrel, compared with the repertoire of our little passengers, sounded like the Salvation Army. After a bit the bus driver drew up, and complained that he might be a married man with children but he refused to drive any further unless they toned it down a bit. Then fortunately, three of the girls were sick all at once, and this quieted the rest down until we breasted the South Downs and saw Whortleton spread below us, with its usual appearance of a pile of smoking rubble tipped beside the sparkling sea.

"Dear old Whortleton," observed Squiffy, recovering from his dose of hashish. "Quite charming."

"At this distance you don't get the smell of the chips and sewage," I reminded him. "Not to mention the jukeboxes and the trippers screaming up and down the roller coaster."

The holiday camp had been built on a reclaimed refuse dump outside the town, and looked just like any other holiday camp you see on the posters all summer—the Lucullus Dining Hall, the Mediterranean Swimming Pool, the Jive Dive, the Darby and Joan Snuggery, rows of red and yellow chalets, and chaps in funny hats going about slapping people on the back to make sure they were happy.

We stopped at a gate in the high wire fence, plastered with the news that Basil Beauchamp was appearing on Saturday in Person. Our pocket Amazons, making a sudden recovery from the emesis, slid back the door and dashed for the red and yellow buildings screaming, apparently for men.

"Is this the only gate in the camp?" I asked the guard chap.

"That's right, mate."

"If any of my little friends try to get out of it, clock them with the nozzle of your fire hose. Come, Squiffy. After all that marijuana I feel I want a bit of a quiet lie-down."

Squiffy and I found our chalet, but we'd hardly time to test the beds and wonder who'd left behind a black bra and a pair of brown boots, before there was a knock on the door and a military-looking cove in a blue blazer appeared.

"Dr. Grimsdyke? I am the Camp Commandant."

"Oh, how d'you do . . . sir."

"Look here, this won't do at all. This party you've brought down from London. They've already wrecked the Olde Tyme Tudor Bar and upset the Fish and Chiperie, and now they're chasing a lot of young men up and down the Mickey Mouse Golf Course. Also," he added, "one is being sick into the swimming pool."

"All right," I told him wearily. "I'll do my best. Perhaps we'd better start with the little vomiter," I suggested, putting professional things first.

The patient at the pool turned out to be Lady Chatterley's friend, the one with the acne.

"I was took queer," she explained.

"Why the devil can't you take queer in the proper place, like everyone else?"

"I feel proper poorly."

"I bet you do. Everyone does after too much gin at lunch time."

"I don't arf itch."

I took another look.

"How many of these spots are permanent features?" I asked.

"Wassay?"

I turned to the Commandant. "I don't suppose you've got a camp hospital, have you? With an isolation ward?"

"Of course we have, Doctor, we have all facilities here. We use it quite a bit at each end of the season."

"I mean, it really is isolated? Barbed wire fence all round? Good. How about nurses?"

"We are lucky enough to employ two former sisters from the Army Medical Service."

"And I expect you've got one or two hefty chaps among your back-slappers? Ex-commandos? Wrestlers enjoying a summer letup?"

"We have three or four former members of the Military Police on our staff, certainly."

"Well, you can put the lot in charge of the isolation hut."

"What! To control one little girl?"

I shook my head. "This patient has German measles, but I'm putting the rest of the party in strict quarantine. Now if you can rustle up a few cricket bats and a length of stout rope, we'll admit the cases to hospital."

Chapter Twenty-Four

"This is the life," said Squiffy approvingly from his deck chair. He stretched out his legs, encased in pepper-and-salt trousers, an old pair of tennis shoes, and one red and one black sock. "Bags of sunshine, fish and chips twice a day, and nothing to do except watch them play off the heats for Saturday afternoon's beauty contest. I much prefer it to the Carlton at Cannes."

"Things are certainly more restful since we got those brats in the cooler," I agreed.

It was a couple of afternoons later, and we sat beside the Plage-o-Drome while I got on with my Boswell's *Johnson*. I'd always the ambition to read it all the way through, and I still had another six hundred and eighty-four pages to go.

Squiffy scratched his head. "I say, Grim—don't you think we're being rather hard on the little ones?"

"*We* are being hard on *them?*"

"They were a bit high-spirited to begin with, I agree. But what's the seaside for if it isn't high spirits? The little dears ought to be playing happily with the rubber ducks on the Kiddies' Heaven."

"They'd be much more likely playing happily with the fruit machines in the Tankard Tavern. Besides, they'd be infecting everyone within spitting distance."

"But when I borrowed your key and went to have a chat with

the kiddiwinks after breakfast, they said they'd all had German measles except that one."

"I isolated them," I said firmly. "And they jolly well stay isolated until I say so."

"I dunno, Grim." Squiffy scratched his head again. "I just can't understand you these days. You used to be such a bright and happy character, and now you might be old Job himself sitting sunning his boils. You don't even seem interested in those lovely girls in the beauty competition."

I'd noticed the girls wandering round the camp, guarded by a pack of rather sinister chaps. But for years all girls in beauty competitions had struck me as looking like a row of new Bentleys, shiny, expensive, nice to possess, but all exactly alike.

"Between you and me, Grim, I've absolutely picked the winner," Squiffy went on warmly. "It's that girl called Pagan Flame. She's got all the points—lovely thighs, good deep chest, healthy hair, not to mention terrific stamina."

"Yes, I noticed that you'd been hanging round the stabling."

"Got to keep an eye on the fancy, Grim. Someone might nobble her. You know, puncture her bra, or something."

"Hi, there, Georgie-Porgie!"

At that moment Pagan Flame herself appeared round the corner of the Bingo Hall, wearing a black swimsuit.

"Why, hello," returned Squiffy, blinking a bit.

"How's my cave man this morning?" She laughed, slapping him on the shoulder and knocking his glasses off.

Pagan Flame was an Australian, a tall good-looking redhead of the sort who look so smashing lying all bronzed on the Sydney beaches. She was just the chum for one of those life-guards who drag in a couple of swimmers with one hand while beating off the sharks with the other, but her general effect on Squiffy was making him look like a cornfield just vacated by a herd of elephants.

"Still working out how to blow up the world, Georgie-

Porgie?" She grinned, giving him a pinch that pretty well amputated his arm.

"Turning over a few formulas in my head, you know. I'll be along to the Dubarry Ballroom as soon as they sound the fanfare on the Tannoy."

"Just you watch for my wiggle." Pagan Flame laughed again, blowing a kiss and striding off.

"Interesting girl, that," said Squiffy.

"And yet another you've led up the garden path of the Atomic Energy Authority?"

"Grim, you *are* a spoilsport. Honestly, you're like my old man when the bank rate goes up during his lumbago. Everyone shoots a bit of a line in these places, anyway. I impressed her no end in the Bingo Bar last night, holding forth about the new bomb. You know, the really jolly one that knocks everybody off but leaves the homes and gardens. The opposition just moves in and takes over the lot, Marble Arch, Crown Jewels, and all."

"Where did you get all that from, may I ask?"

"The science mag I confiscated from one of the brats at the prepper, but she wasn't to know. And a jolly shrewd move it turned out," Squiffy continued. "There was a fellow called Whitherspoon or something at the bar, who turned out to be a bookie enjoying his seaside fortnight." He laughed. "Odd, Grim, isn't it, you never think of bookies having holidays? Difficult to imagine them at all without their little blackboard and that leather satchel bursting at the seams with the takings. Still, I suppose they have wives and families and are kind to dogs, like ordinary people. That fellow Whitherspoon," ended Squiffy proudly, "took me for a mug."

"Go on?" I remarked, reaching for my pocket dominoes.

"Yes, he thought I was some airy-fairy academic type, far too busy blowing everybody up to face the realities of life. So I scraped up absolutely all the cash I could lay hands on and put it on Pagan Flame. And the idiot bookie gave me five to one.

Not bad, eh? I'll pretty well clear off the little amount out-
standing to the head beak."

"But what," I pointed out, "if she doesn't win?"

"But, Grim, she's a cert. I have information."

"Hell is paved with more good tips than good intentions."

"There you go again, Grim. You make Jeremiah sound like
the bloke doing the dog-food commercials on the telly. I
happen to know that Pagan Flame is going to romp past the
post, because Basil told Lucy. All these things have got more
rigging than the entire Whortleton Yacht Squadron, believe
me." A fanfare rang round the camp. "Starter's orders," announced Squiffy, rising. "If you'll excuse me, I must nip along
and get myself a good place on the rails."

I turned back to my Boswell. Then I had a go at the
dominoes, but you'd be surprised how unexciting it is playing
dominoes by yourself. Squiffy was right, of course. If I'd
found myself among the prophets of doom, they'd be rallying
round trying to cheer me up with funny stories. I began to
wonder if I were incubating something like jaundice or a de-
pressive psychosis. Why, I asked myself, was I seeing life
through the yellow filter, when in less than a fortnight I
should be marrying the nicest girl in the world? I ought to be
indistinguishable from one of the camp's band of backslappers.

I gazed out to sea and tried to cheer myself up by picturing
the future. We should have a nice house in a nice suburb and
Dame Hilda would fix me up with a nice medical job in one of
her welfare organizations. Anemone would keep me nice and
clean and cook me a nice dinner every night and we should
have lots of nice children. Besides, I was jolly lucky getting a
mother-in-law who could organize half-a-dozen homes for
delinquent females as easily as organizing her spring cleaning.
From the morning's post Dame Hilda had already arranged the
wedding down to the last silver-paper horseshoe, and even
saved me the sweat of booking the honeymoon by fixing us up

with a chum who ran a home for unmarried mothers in Scotland. And dear old Miles, of course, would choke with delight over his wedding cake, feeling the match made him and Dame Hilda pretty well blood brothers.

I pocketed the dominoes. I felt a change of scene might be curative.

I strolled through the camp gate and wandered into Whortleton. I bought a plate of jellied eels. I leant over the rails on the prom. There, I noticed, was the very spot I tackled the bee on Lucy's neck. There was our romantic outfall. Those senile donkeys were probably the very ones on which I softened her up with free rides. I gave another of those sighs. Whenever I bit a stick of Whortleton rock, to me it would always have LUCY in letters all the way through.

I treated myself to a lobster tea, a go at the shooting gallery, and the full program at the local cinema. It was getting late when I reached our chalet, and Squiffy still being out I climbed into bed, had another go at Boswell, and quietly dropped off.

I was shaken awake by Squiffy about two in the morning.

"Hey! Grim! Congratulate me."

"What have you done? Scooped the bingo pool?"

"No, I'm going to be married."

He started marching up and down the chalet, arms and legs banging against the fittings.

"I've just proposed to little Audrey. Out there beside the Seaview Skittle Alley. And she accepted me."

"Audrey? Who's Audrey?"

"Audrey Urridge. That's Pagan Flame's real name."

I rubbed my eyes. "You don't mean to say you've actually suggested—?"

"Why not? I love her. She has great strength of character, a very affectionate nature, and beautiful teeth."

"Look, Squiffy—why don't you get a bit of sleep now and we'll sort all this out calmly in the morning."

"Mind you, it wasn't a push-over," Squiffy continued. "Far from it. Audrey said, 'Go on, Cobber, I hardly know you, and I don't mix with professors anyway.' So I said I wasn't really a professor—I'd promoted myself a bit during the evening, I suppose—I was merely the worthless only son of a bloke who owned half a bank in the city, and she said, Correction, please, she'd marry me any day I liked. What do you think of that?"

"As far as I am concerned," I told him, lying down again, "you can ruddy well marry all twelve finalists and Basil Beauchamp as well."

"There you go, Grim. You're like Scrooge missing the four aways again on his football pools. Most people sound jolly pleased when other people tell them they're engaged."

"I'm sure your old man will make up for it when he gets back from Karachi next week."

"I've thought of that." Squiffy sat on his bed. "The old man is certainly a bit cagey about my affairs. He's had to buy off a few girls from time to time, and now he's definitely out of the market. But with Audrey it's different. So I'm going to show my dad and the entire world what a terrific chap I am by nabbing this sinister spy chap, Yarmouth."

"What, the comrade from Notting Hill?"

"That's it. I'm not at all satisfied with Lucy's explanation. After all, if Audrey and the bookie and you thought I was a high-class scientist, why shouldn't he?"

"Good night," I said, rolling over.

"I've still got Noreen's phone number, so tomorrow I'll get in touch and tell him to send the onion bloke down to Whortleton on Saturday night. I'll say I've got some absolutely terrific secrets on the transfer list, at rock-bottom prices."

"Good night."

"And jolly silly he's going to look waiting by the floral clock, when I march up with half the Whortleton police force on my heels. Particularly, of course, with all those onions."

"Good night."

"You really are being an old frosty-face, Grim. It wasn't a bit like this the last time we were at Whortleton. I don't care what you say, I shall finally unmask Yarmouth and get all sorts of medals at Buckingham Palace and put the old man in a wonderful mood and get him to let me marry Pagan Flame. So there."

"Good night."

I wondered what dear Lucy would say if she found her dear brother all over the morning papers, battered to death with Boswell.

Chapter Twenty-Five

The Saturday of the beauty finals was another jolly lovely Whortleton day, with the sun sparkling happily on the silvery sands beside the bright blue sea, the gay little white boats bobbing about, and the pretty little yellow helicopter buzzing above dragging out the people caught by the undertow.

"And how are the dear little chickabiddies today?" asked Squiffy, returning from queueing up at the cafeteria for his seconds of sausages at breakfast.

"In rather good form at my morning visit," I told him. "Quite respectful for once."

My reception in the isolation hut was usually that of King Herod the Great at the local Mothers' Union. But that Saturday the little girls were all looking clean and tidy in their white dresses and bobbing curtsies all round.

"A week in isolation has done them no end of good," I suggested. "Taken their minds off being teen-agers for a bit, I suppose. It must be terrible having to go round all the time remembering what a shocking problem you are."

"Well, this is the great day." Squiffy helped himself to more tomato sauce. "They're off at two-thirty, and it'll be a proud moment for me when I'm leading Pagan Flame into the Bingo Bar as the winner. I've never seen a woman in better condition. She's moving well, full of spirit, and taking her food wonderfully. A girl of great talent, Audrey." Squiffy reached for the marmalade. "Did you know she can sing and do jolly funny imitations of girls performing the belly dance in the Casbah?"

"That should be one way of getting through your long domestic evenings."

"Besides, she's bags of badinage and funny Australian jokes. Though the language is a bit of a snag sometimes. I always thought a wombat was something they played cricket with." Squiffy looked at his watch. "This Beauchamp perisher is turning up after lunch, I suppose. Though it'll be nice to see old Lucy again."

"Yes, it will be nice to see old Lucy again."

"Look here, Grim," suggested Squiffy, "you're so down in the mouth these days you need taking out of yourself. Next Saturday, when we're all back in town, how about you and I and Lucy and Pagan making up a foursome? We can go on a picnic somewhere with a hamper absolutely stuffed with food, and end up with a bite of dinner at a quiet spot on the river. I can easily play host, of course, on Pagan's winnings. What do you say?"

"Next Saturday I'm afraid I've got an engagement."

"Oh, rotten luck. I just thought it might be fun. I suppose we'll have to take that Beauchamp bird instead. I'd better nip along and see Pagan," Squiffy ended, wiping up the remains of the tomato sauce with his bread and marmalade. "She always breakfasts in bed, to conserve her strength. Sure you wouldn't like to put a bit on her, too? Though I don't suppose Whitherspoon now would give you better than evens."

He hurried off, leaving me prodding my scrambled egg. I seemed to be losing my appetite. Like Miles and everyone else in the profession I'm a bit of a hypochondriac, and I wondered if I were cooking up some really nasty complaint. Then they'd have to postpone the wedding, I reflected solemnly. The invitations would be canceled, the presents put in the attic, the vicar given the afternoon off, the cake cut up and distributed to the poor.

"The poor chap," everyone would say. "Languishing in some beastly hospital when he should be having a jolly time of it getting married." There I'd be, behind screens at the end of the ward, all pale, with Anemone holding my hand, the nurses passing on tiptoe and the consultant outside scratching his head and saying, "Tell George to be sure to get a post-mortem."

I suddenly realized I'd finished my scrambled egg and was feeling rather more cheerful.

"Grim!" Squiffy burst through the Dining Hall doors. "Grim! Come at once. It's Pagan. She's coughing."

"Oh, yes?"

"Worse than that, she looks all peculiar. She's lying in bed crying her eyes out and saying she wishes she were back in Australia."

"Peculiar? How do you mean, peculiar?"

"All red and blotchy and hot to the touch."

"Oh, she's got German measles," I told him. "I'd better go and have a look."

"A pink macular rash," I was observing in her chalet a few minutes later. "On the face and spreading to the trunk. Ah, yes. Do you itch, Miss Flame?"

"I feel lousy all over."

"That's right. General malaise, coryza, slight conjunctival injection. Temperature's up, of course. May I feel behind the ears? As I thought. Enlargement of the posterior cervical and suboccipital glands." I replaced the stricken beauty's head on the pillow. "Never had German measles before? Rubella it is, then. Lot of it about this summer."

"But what are you going to do, Grim?" demanded Squiffy, jumping about at the bedside.

"Nothing, old lad. There isn't any treatment. I'll tell the Camp Commandant you'll be in dock for a few days, Miss Flame. Take plenty of fluids and don't worry. Good morning."

"But the beauty contest," hissed Squiffy, as soon as we stepped outside.

"I've never heard of a girl winning a beauty contest covered with spots."

"But if she's scratched I'll lose my cash."

"So you will, Squiffy. Too bad."

"But damn it, Grim!" Squiffy held his head with both hands. "I've laid a thousand quid with Whitherspoon on that woman."

I stared at the chap. "A thousand quid? But you never had anything like that sort of cash hanging about. You haven't been burgling your own bank, have you?"

"Not exactly. But I thought I was on such a cert, if I could really collect a packet I'd not only pay off the head beak but snap my fingers at the old man, should by any chance he raise objections to my marrying Audrey. Then I noticed this terribly sporty offer in the personal column of the local paper."

"You're not entering for the cross-channel race?"

"No, there are some coves with an office round the back of the Town Hall, who apparently think it a crying shame chaps like me with fathers bursting with cash should go about with hardly enough to keep body and soul on the same spot. So they just let you have the stuff on tick until convenient. A very useful arrangement all round. A wonder a lot of other people haven't thought of it. They were all for giving me five thousand once they'd established who I was, but I'm a pretty careful bird in many respects, Grim, and kept it down to one. And now—oh, gosh!"

"Look here, you idiot. I'm sure this sort of bet isn't recognized at Tattersall's. You can get this Whitherspoon to give you your stake back again."

Squiffy gazed at me. "Have you ever known anyone anywhere to get their money back out of a bookie?"

"You have a point," I agreed.

"Can't you give her something, Grim?" he pleaded. "Surely

you medical coves these days have all sorts of wonder drugs up your sleeves?"

"German measles isn't in the wonder drug class."

"But damn it! How on earth did she catch it in the first place?"

"From the kid who was sick in the swimming bath, I suppose. Five days is just about in the incubation period."

"I'm going to chuck myself off the pier," announced Squiffy.

"Yes, I suppose that's about the best thing you could do," I told him, not only thoroughly fed up with the chump but having worries enough of my own.

I strode back to the chalet to prepare a nice little speech for next Saturday's wedding. As I'd already lined up the Ascot outfit from Mr. Moss and his invaluable brothers, and as Dame Hilda had bought the ring and sent me the bill from Asprey's, this was all that remained for me to contribute to the proceedings. I sat down at the bedside table with a sheet of paper. As I remembered from acting as second on these occasions, the happy bridegroom first brought merry chuckles all round by referring to "My wife," then he thanked all the uncles and aunts for the cut glass and silverware, and ended up with a funny story to leave them in tucks over the champers. I went on staring at the paper. For the life of me I couldn't think of a funny story. Even the one about the bishop and the parrot, which, cleaned up a bit, might do, seemed to have gone from my mind like last week's cricket scores. I sat smoking cigarettes and gazing at the happy campers cavorting in the sunshine. But of course, I was happier than any of them. Lucky me was shortly going to marry the nicest, etc.

I was interrupted by the reappearance of Squiffy.

"Grim," he announced. "I am a changed man."

"Oh, yes?"

"Totally." He sat on the bed and twisted his legs. "A few

minutes ago I was about to end it all by chucking myself off the top board into the swimming pool."

"I thought it was going to be the pier?"

"Yes, but the pool's heated," Squiffy explained. "No point in being uncomfortable about it, is there? As I gazed in the swirling waters beneath I suddenly saw the error of my ways."

I picked up my pencil. I fancied I'd once heard a funny story about an old lady and a bus conductor, and wondered if that might do.

"Here am I," Squiffy continued. "Born with every advantage a child could want, including a wise father who saw the folly of placing in my youthful hands the agent of dissipation and self-destruction. I refer, of course, to the rhino."

I lit another cigarette.

"Instead, my thoughtful pa placed in those hands the very key to the universe—the key of science. I'm quoting from that magazine I confiscated. And what did I do, Grim? I burnt the ruddy lab down, that's what I did. I'm a fool."

I agreed.

"Now I'm going straight back to Mireborough to beg forgiveness, and I'm going to work like stink and get a degree and benefit humanity. I might take up medicine after all, Grim. Are there any beastly medical jobs still going? Leper colonies, and so on?"

I doodled a bit on the paper.

"I should like now, Grim, to give a little talk to the girls on the subject. I feel they would find it very improving."

"I'm sure they would."

"I think they, too, might see the errors of their ways, and all go home and sing in the choir."

"Possibly."

"And so, Grim, if you will kindly let me have your key to the isolation hospital—"

"There you are," I told the chap shortly. "Now for heaven's sake clear off. I'm busy."

"Thank you, Grim. Beside their little beds at night, for years to come, they will bless your heart. Just you wait and see."

Squiffy left. I sat over the paper, smoking more cigarettes and wondering what on earth it was the bishop said to that parrot, and vice versa.

Chapter Twenty-Six

∿

By lunch time everyone in the camp was becoming pretty excited at the prospect of seeing Basil Beauchamp. I was even feeling pretty excited myself. Which was odd, as I'd never been excited at the prospect of seeing Basil, even when we shared digs and he'd just got a part, which held out hope of his re-paying my small advances.

I hadn't noticed Squiffy at lunch, which was odd as well, because I'd never known him to miss his fish and chips. Feeling that he had decided to start his new life with a fast, or even, with luck, that he'd decided to chuck himself off the pier after all, I dismissed the chap from mind and went to join the mob waiting for Basil's car to appear through the camp gate.

Actually, it was Lucy's little Aston Martin that appeared. With an escort of backslappers she drove slowly through the girls, who were trying to kiss the windshield, toward the Dubarry Ballroom. Basil stepped out and gave his famous smile, everyone started screaming, photo bulbs flashed, a couple of girls fainted at the front, and he was whisked toward the stage door at the back.

Lucy was left sitting behind the steering wheel. Nobody seemed to take any notice of her at all.

"Lucy, old girl," I cried, making my way through the mob, which was chanting for Basil to come out and kiss it.

"Why, Gaston!" Her face brightened as she wound down the window. "Enjoying your holiday?"

"Holiday? Good lord, it's no holiday. Hard-working stuff, you know, child welfare. Infectious diseases to treat, and so on."

"I'm sorry you had to leave town so suddenly."

"So was I. But I had to help out a professional chum. We doctors, you know. Got to stick together. How was Lord's?"

"Oh, fine. Basil canceled an engagement and took me."

"And Glyndebourne?"

"Oh, fine. Basil took me there too."

She switched off her engine.

"Of course," I added through the window, "it's not only the opera, it's the lovely surroundings."

"The surroundings? Oh, I didn't really see much of the surroundings. Since Basil's new film has been released, you never see much of anything at all when you're with him. Except a sea of admiring faces, all looking exactly alike except for the expense of their makeup."

The mob started chanting "Basil!" over and over again, as though the chap were doing something really useful, like converting tries at Twickenham.

"It's tough luck on these posh actors," I observed. "No private life. Fans everywhere. Recognized at once, whether it's L'Ecu de France or the local. Jolly hard on Basil having to put up with it."

"I think Basil puts up with it perfectly splendidly," said Lucy briefly. "Where's my brother?"

"I don't know. He announced his intention of taking a swim from the pier."

"Who? George? But he won't even take a bath unless the water's boiling."

"The sea air seems to have made a bit of a change in him. Shall we go in and grab some seats for the show? It looks like being a full house."

We found Squiffy already sitting in the front row beside the little stage, which was all flags and flowers and with a special curtain at the back on a silken rope for Basil to pull.

"What ho, Lucy," he greeted his sister cheerfully. "I was just bagging three nice gangway seats. Don't you think I've caught the sun?"

"Your nose is peeling rather disgustingly, if that's what you mean."

"Let's make ourselves comfy. You don't see the finals of a national beauty contest every day of the week, do you?"

"You seem to have perked up a good bit," I remarked, as he settled down between Lucy and myself.

"You can't stay long in the dumps at a jolly place like this, Grim."

"You mean you got your cash back from Whitherspoon?"

"Of course not." Squiffy grinned. "A bet's a bet, isn't it?"

There was a fanfare over the Tannoy, and to the accompaniment of general mania, Basil took the stage.

"Mums and dads, boys and girls," started our film star. "I hope you're as pleased to see me as I am to see you."

Cries of "Yes!" "You betcher!" and "Ain't he lovely close to?"

"We actors," continued Basil, who somehow managed to orate while keeping a fixed grin on his face, "have many duties to our public. I don't shirk them, boys and girls. I love them. Because I love my public."

This brought such a din from the audience I hardly noticed the Camp Commandant tapping my shoulder.

"Mr. Beauchamp is better, then?" he asked, looking worried.

"Better?"

"I got your message, Doctor. To say he'd suddenly been taken ill and to hold up the contest for half an hour."

"My message—?"

"I love you all," Basil went on. "That's why I'm so delighted to be with you this beautiful afternoon in this simply delicious camp at this charming resort of Whortleton. Now I'm not going to waste any more of my time—any more of your time —before judging the finals of this exciting beauty contest. I only hope, mums and dads and boys and girls, that when I pull this cord to reveal the lovely ladies, you won't completely forget me while blinded by their breath-taking beauty."

Basil tugged the silken rope. He certainly revealed a dozen girls in their swimsuits striking provocative postures. But instead of the official beauties they were our maladjusted teenagers.

"What the devil—" choked Basil.

The audience was sandbagged into a mystified silence.

"Fixture canceled," hissed Squiffy, digging me in the ribs. "See, I get my money back."

But I couldn't cotton onto this before Lucy started to laugh.

"Lucy!" snapped Basil over the hyacinths. "I demand to know who is making a fool of me."

I gave a bit of a guffaw myself. Squiffy giggled. And laughter being more infectious than cholera, in a shake the whole hall was roaring its head off.

"Who is responsible for these monstrosities?" demanded Basil angrily.

The girls just stood grinning, thinking it all no end of a prank. Basil tugged the silken rope and found it operated only in one direction. I sat wiping my eyes. Though I saw the poor chap's point. Any actor would rather be smeared with treacle and eaten alive by giant ants than made to look ridiculous in public.

"Get these girls away from here!" Basil stamped his foot. "Is there no one in the entire beastly place responsible for them?"

"Yes, young man," said Dame Hilda, advancing down the gangway with Anemone. "I am."

I jumped up. "Good lord, Dame Hilda! What on earth are you doing down here?"

"Doing here? But you sent a telegram last night saying all my girls were seriously ill in hospital."

"Oh, did I?"

"'E's bin cruel to us," shouted the girl with acne, pointing in my direction. "Proper cruel. 'E ought to be inside, 'e ought."

"What exactly is going on, if you please?" demanded Dame Hilda, mounting the stage.

"Do you know who I am?" asked Basil furiously.

"I do not, young man, nor do I care. I only wish to discover who is responsible for submitting my girls to this ghastly exhibition."

"'E locked us up," screamed the girl with the strabismus.

"On bleedin' bread and water," added Lady Chatterley.

"For God's sake let down the curtain, somebody," appealed Basil.

"Dr. Grimsdyke," commanded Dame Hilda, after all that telly unabashed at being watched by a couple of hundred startled campers. "Come here instantly."

I looked round wildly for support. There was only Squiffy, and from the look on his face he seemed to have switched off his brain at the mains.

"Gaston, darling," said Lucy loudly. "Who on earth is this peculiar woman? Do you actually know her?"

"How dare you!" snapped Dame Hilda, going pink. "That happens to be the man who is going to marry my daughter."

Lucy gasped. "Gaston! You never told me."

"Oh, sorry, Lucy." I felt a bit conspicuous, in front of all those people, with the edge of my soul showing. "It sort of slipped my memory, I suppose."

"Play the national anthem," called Basil despairingly. "Sound the fire alarm."

"Who might you be, young woman?" snapped Dame Hilda.

"Don't you 'young woman' me," Lucy snapped back, jumping to her feet. "I happen to have been a particularly close friend of Gaston's practically all my life."

"Gaston!" Dame Hilda gave the glare that set delinquents back on their stiletto heels. "Have you the temerity to conduct another affair behind my back?"

"Ladies and gentlemen," announced Basil, mopping himself with a silk handkerchief. "That, I'm afraid concludes our little performance for this afternoon—"

"You have besmirched the honor of my daughter!"

"Oh, have I, Dame Hilda?" Then something happened. I suddenly felt Lucy slip her hand into mine. "I have not besmirched your daughter's ruddy honor," I went on, throwing out the chest a bit. "Come to think of it, I've only kissed her when you've been looking on to see fair play."

"Have you taken leave of your senses, man? You will come back to Yorkshire with me at once."

"No, I won't."

"Yes, you will."

"Don't you argue with me."

"I'll jolly well argue with anyone I feel like."

"I am absolutely sick and tired of this," said someone in the background.

With a bit of a shock I saw it was Anemone.

"Anemone! Have you taken leave of your wits, too?"

"On the contrary, Mummy, I have just returned to them. I have been goaded absolutely beyond measure by you and Gaston and everyone else who's been running my life these past two years."

I stared at my fiancée. I'd never seen her looking like it before. She was all flowing blonde hair, flashing blue eyes, and jutting little chin. The fact was, the poor girl had come to the end of her psychological countdown.

"Anemone, my girl! Stop it at once, I say."

"It must have been horrifyingly obvious to absolutely every-one between here and Yorkshire," Anemone went on, "except you, of course, Mummy, that Gaston and I haven't the slightest desire to marry each other. He thinks I'm simply dreary, and personally I think he's no end of a drip."

I didn't care much for the drip bit, but I suddenly felt my-self warming to the conversation.

"Anemone, you will do as I say at once."

"I am not, Mummy, one of your delinquents. I have done as you said all my life, Mummy. If I did as you said now, Mummy, and married a man who interests me about as much as the racing tips in the daily papers, whose conversation entertains me about as much as a Saturday-night comedian on the Light Programme, whose moral stature I respect about as much as a secondhand car salesman, and whose earning capacity strikes me as rather inferior to a well-trained village idiot—if I did, I should be damned now and forever."

"I intend, my girl, to give you a thorough talking to—"

"If you wish, Mummy, you may tear me limb from limb. You may submit me to any sort of mental or moral torture you happen to feel inclined. But as for marrying that man gorping at us over the potted plants, I would let you burn me alive first."

The audience broke into a round of applause.

"Young lady!" Basil clutched her. "Can you sing?"

Anemone looked rather taken aback, but said, "Yes, I've been told I have quite a nice voice."

"Such fire! Such presence! Such looks! Such dignity, such diction! Ladies and gentlemen—" Basil drew Anemone toward the footlights. "This afternoon is the proudest in my life. After months of searching among amateur dramatic societies and provincial repertories up and down the country, I have at last found her. Ladies and gentlemen—allow me to present the young unknown who will—subject, of course, to audition, contract, and my commission as her personal agent—have the honor of playing opposite myself in the forthcoming production of Shaw's immortal play *Saint Joan*, shortly opening in London as a musical under the title of *My Fair Lady of Orleans*."

This brought terrific cheers from the audience, who were beginning to feel the whole afternoon much better than the pierrots. I hardly noticed the Camp Commandant come up again to announce in an even more worried voice, "Doctor, the police have come for your friend."

"That's him," shouted a youth with a moustache and large glasses, hurrying down the aisle with a couple of Whortleton coppers. "That's the blighter. Not content with trying to sneak my girl, he's betraying the secrets of his country, that's what. Traitor! Turncoat! Renegade! Rat!"

"Here, I say," protested Squiffy. "You've got it wrong. I'm not the traitor. You are, dash it."

"Tried to seduce my Noreen, you did."

Squiffy stared. "Look, comrade, I can explain everything—"

"Comrade! Called me comrade, did you? That proves it, doesn't it, officer? Me, a pillar of the Young Conservatives."

"I think you'd better come along to the station, sir," invited the leading rozzer.

Squiffy started arguing with the policemen. Dame Hilda started arguing with Basil. And everyone in the hall suddenly seemed to start arguing with each other.

"Retarded," said Lucy in my ear.

"Eh?"

"Retarded. I have all my life been trying to hit on the right word to describe my brother. At last I have it." She looked round calmly. "Gaston, dear, my car is outside. Shall we go?"

"Go? But how about Basil?"

"Basil?" said Lucy simply. "Why, Basil can walk."

Chapter Twenty-Seven

∿

The sun was stretching out the Welsh hills and the shadows had started putting up the shutters for the day across the tumbling waters of the River Usk. It was approaching that magic moment on a summer's evening when the flies hatch from the water like smoke and big fish plop with befitting dignity in sun-forsaken pools, when fishermen throw out their chests and raise their rods and thank heaven for allowing its creatures such a beautiful world to dwell in, before trying to remove as many fish as possible from it before supper.

"Poor Gaston," murmured Lucy, dropping into third as her Aston rounded a corner.

"Mostly my fault, I suppose," I admitted. "Come to think of it, I've been a bit of a mutt."

"Yes, you have rather, haven't you?" Lucy agreed cheerfully. "But you possess such a sweet nature, Gaston."

"Oh, come—"

"You'll always do anything for anybody. You let people push you around quite unthinkingly, like a revolving door."

"Oh, tut—"

"That cousin of yours, for instance." I'd told Lucy the whole story during the cross-country journey. "You ought to stand up to him, Gaston. Stamp on his toes and spit in his eye."

"Difficult to spit in the eye of a chap who once gave you

six of the best, just because he'd found you with a pot of strawberry jam under the bedclothes."

"What a pity, Gaston," Lucy continued, "you had no one at your side to support you against these people."

"It was, I suppose."

"Someone with strength of character."

"True enough."

"And with a mind of their own."

"Exactly."

We turned another corner.

"Aren't we getting near the place?" asked Lucy.

I glanced at the river runing beside the road.

"I can't see the old boy anywhere."

"You're sure he won't mind? I mean, our just arriving like this?"

"Since I got him out of clink in New York I don't think he'd mind if I arrived at midnight with a traveling circus. Besides, he's got bags of room. He usually runs a businessmen's clinic, but that's closed at the moment."

Lucy sighed.

"After this afternoon, if I don't have a week lying low and completely away from it all, I shall go as mad as my brother."

"I'm a bit worried about old George," I confessed. "After all, we did rather leave him in the clutches of the law."

"If they lock him up, Father will unlock him when he gets home next week. Though I shouldn't think any self-respecting jail would put up with George as long as that."

"Here's the house," I announced, as Sir Lancelot's front gates came in sight.

I was a bit surprised to find the gates shut, with barbed wire along the top and a large red notice saying KEEP OUT.

"The old boy may have sold up, I suppose," I suggested, feeling pretty mystified as I left the car to investigate.

The gates being unlocked, I swung them open for Lucy to drive inside. I was about to climb in again, when Sir Lancelot himself bobbed up among the shrubbery.

"Good evening, Grimsdyke," he said, very genially. "An unexpected pleasure, is it not?"

"Oh, good evening, sir." I stood staring at him.

"Is this a social call? Or do you intend to stay?"

"Well, I—er, I was rather thinking of asking you to put us up for a few days, sir. But then I didn't quite foresee—"

"You have a companion? Come out, young lady. I shall not eat you. Indeed, I remember you. I never forget a face or an abdomen. I once advised, at considerable expense to your family, that your father have his stomach removed and that you have your tonsils removed. I believe nothing came of either suggestion."

"Good evening, Sir Lancelot. No it didn't, I'm afraid," replied Lucy calmly.

"A waste of money, you see." Sir Lancelot sniffed a rose he happened to be carrying. "I am at last realizing the laughable unimportance of money and the outward trappings of this world. A beautiful evening, is it not?"

"Perhaps you may find it a trifle chilly, sir?" I suggested.

"Not quite yet. A little later perhaps." Sir Lancelot paused to listen to the birds. "Charming. Just like your earlier visit, Grimsdyke."

It was, except that this time Sir Lancelot had no clothes on.

"A return to Nature, Grimsdyke. There is nothing like it for physical and mental health. I hit upon the idea while seeing my wife off for a Scandinavian holiday earlier in the week. I fancy she will feel perfectly at home when she returns. Of course my sunshine clinic is hardly yet under way, but I am sure we shall see many well-known bodies here before the snows of next winter. You two may, of course, stay as long as you like as my guests."

"I think, sir, that we'd better be getting on—"

"As this is a clinic and not a camp, I separate the sexes during the day. We dress for dinner."

"The arrangement suits us perfectly, Sir Lancelot," said Lucy. "We've no luggage anyway."

"Very good my dear. Perhaps you would proceed in the other direction and report to the matron? Grimsdyke, you will come with me. We can still enjoy a pleasant game of basketball with the others before dusk."

"Look here, Lucy—I mean, you're not really serious—?"

"Of course I am, Gaston. I always try anything once. Besides, what have I got to worry about, with my figure?"

"Come along, Grimsdyke."

"Lucy—"

"Yes, Gaston?"

I swallowed. "Lucy, there's something I've simply got to tell you."

"Yes, Gaston?"

"That bee. On your neck. It was one of the sort that don't sting."

"I know, Gaston. I looked it up in the bee book. But I never let it make the slightest difference to us."

"Come, Grimsdyke! Make haste."

I wandered toward the shrubbery, removing my sports jacket.

I turned back. "Lucy—"

"Yes, Gaston?"

"Lucy, I haven't got much of a job."

"I'll persuade Daddy to give you one. Running his Medical Foundation, for instance."

"But your father hasn't got a Medical Foundation."

"I'll persuade him to found one. It'd be very much easier than persuading him to put money into Basil's beastly musical."

"If you please, Grimsdyke," commanded Sir Lancelot.

I took off my tie. "Coming, sir."

I reached the cover of the bushes.

"Lucy," I called. "Will you marry me?"

"Of course, darling," called Lucy back.

"The psychology of clothing," observed Sir Lancelot, with another sniff at his rose, "which has been thoroughly investigated by Krafft-Ebbing, presents several highly interesting psychiatric hypotheses. It is, of course, bound up with the taboo complex, ingrained in all of us from the moment our maternity nurse puts on our first pair of baby's nappies. In this manner we first become conditioned to certain areas automatically creating a sense of shame and anxiety . . ."

I stumbled happily into the sunset, removing my trousers.